LETHAL BETRAYAL

VANISHING RANCH
BOOK 5

CHRISTY BARRITT

CHAPTER 1

The sweltering landscape blurred around Emily Holcomb as she staggered forward.

"Keep moving," she murmured to herself. "You've got to keep moving."

She took another step, the motion taking entirely more energy than it should.

As despair began to set in, she licked her dry lips and sang, "Ain't no grave can hold my body down."

She sounded delirious, even to her own ears. But singing always helped calm her.

It reminded her of her determination not to let this desert be her grave—no matter how hard it tried.

Her granddad had loved the old gospel song. For some reason, the lyrics—as well as the memory of her grandad's deep voice as he sang it—brought her comfort and strength now.

Emily paused long enough to suck in a deep breath. Her heart pounded entirely too quickly, and she was hyper-aware of her pulse.

Finding a burst of strength, Emily pulled herself upright and surveyed the area. All she saw in every direction was a sun-bathed, parched desert.

Emily had been walking for hours, and she'd seen the same thing mile after mile. She thought maybe she would've reached one of the mountain ranges surrounding the area by now.

But she hadn't.

She was beginning to doubt she ever would.

Drawing in a breath, she forced herself to walk again. Her swirling head indicated she might fall forward at any minute.

But not if she could help it.

The sun continued to beat down on her. It had to be at least in the high nineties, which seemed unseasonably warm for the desert in October. However, the southwestern part of the United States was experiencing an unprecedented heat wave.

Was that where Emily was? It made the most sense.

But she wasn't sure. She'd been abducted in Los Angeles and had awoken in a strange place she didn't recognize. When she'd seen the opportunity to escape, she'd simply run. Her location made no difference—she only wanted to get away.

Kyle's image flashed in her mind, and Emily sneered.

Anger over the injustice of it all mixed with her fear.

She couldn't give up. First, she needed to bring down those men who preyed on the innocent, who loved wealth more than people.

That was exactly why those men wanted to control her—both out of vengeance for what she'd already done and out of desperation to stop her from ruining any more of their plans.

As Emily's resolve strengthened, she glanced forward.

Something ahead caught her eye, and she squinted.

Was that a . . . person?

Emily blinked and rubbed her eyes.

It almost looked like a man on horseback.

Or was he a desert mirage? Was she seeing things that simply weren't real?

She started to raise her hand and flag him down.

Then another thought hit her: What if that man worked for Arrow?

She froze as panic filled her.

As she turned to run, her head swirled.

She tumbled to the ground and blackness overtook her.

———

Mateo Garcia nudged The Lone Ranger—his black Arabian steed—with the side of his boot as they trotted through the desert. Bouncing over the landscape, his thoughts wandered to the photo he'd gotten via text yesterday.

A photo of his wife.

His deceased wife.

No words had been attached to the image. Just a haunting surveillance-like photo of his beautiful wife as she'd walked down the street of their small Mexican town. Mateo didn't know when or where the picture was taken.

He was only certain the photo had been snapped before she'd been abducted.

Before everything had changed.

Before his life had fallen apart and his heart had been crushed.

Why would someone send Mateo a picture of Rose?

Why now?

Unless the men who'd killed her were out for

blood and it was their way of signaling the coming trouble.

He'd have to figure that out later. For now, he shifted his thoughts back to the present.

More than one resident at Vanishing Ranch had reported seeing people wandering the desert near their property. Most likely, the wanderers were just adventure-seekers exploring the area.

But Mateo had to guard the people residing at the ranch. That meant he and his team had to make sure no strangers—or even worse, enemies—stumbled upon their location. Charlie Soldier, who owned and operated the ranch, had sensors to alert them whenever anyone got too close.

Mateo was mostly doing this out of an abundance of caution.

He continued to trot around the perimeter of the property, ignoring the vultures circling to the east. Something must have died out there. The desert was merciless in so many ways.

Despite the unseasonably hot day, he had to admit it was nice to be out here. He'd always loved horseback riding, and this area reminded him so much of the horse farm in Mexico where he'd grown up.

He'd lived in the United States for the past two years, and Arizona was beginning to feel like home.

He'd known he had to leave Mexico if he truly wanted to heal.

So that's what he'd done.

Something in the distance caught his attention. He pulled the binoculars from his belt and pressed them against his eyes.

He squinted.

What *was* that?

As Mateo got closer to the object, his back muscles tightened.

Was that a . . . person?

"*Vamos!*" He nudged The Lone Ranger to go faster.

His horse burst into a gallop.

The closer they got, the more Mateo's fears were confirmed.

This was . . . a woman.

A woman with curly dark hair, sunburnt skin, and wearing a flowered, knee-length sundress.

Mateo pulled back on the reins, signaling his horse to stop. Then he climbed off and rushed toward her.

Grabbing her shoulders, Mateo shifted her body until her face appeared. Her eyes were closed, her olive skin tinted red from sun exposure, and her lips chapped. Then there were the bruises on her cheek and around one eye. A cut stretched near her chin and another on her forehead.

And her dress . . . it had blood on it. A *lot* of blood.

He quickly checked her pulse and felt a beat.

Her eyes fluttered open a moment.

"Please . . . no . . ." She thrashed on the ground as her words slurred. "I . . . I can't go back there. Don't take me back."

"Take you back where? I'm not going to hurt you."

"Don't let them find me!"

The outburst lasted only a moment before she drifted back into unconsciousness.

Alarmed, Mateo stood and scanned the area. He didn't see anyone.

But that didn't mean no one was near.

Mateo grabbed his phone and called his leader at Vanishing Ranch. He needed a UTV out here.

This woman needed help.

Now.

CHAPTER 2

As soon as they reached the ranch, Mateo scooped the woman from the back of the UTV and rushed her toward the onsite clinic.

"Dr. Cossette is on her way." Charlie hurried beside him, her eyes narrowed as she observed the unconscious woman in his arms. "Did you see anyone else out there?"

"No. Just her." Mateo carried the woman inside, walked with her down a short hallway, and finally reached the clinic area.

Charlie opened the door, and Mateo laid the woman on the hospital bed.

"Looks like you found her just in time." Charlie stepped closer and examined the woman's abdomen and sides.

There were no cuts there.

He was glad the woman wasn't bleeding out. But where had that blood come from?

His gaze slid up to meet Charlie's. "Should we take her to the hospital? Call the sheriff?"

Charlie placed her finger under the woman's jaw to check her pulse. "Her pulse feels strong. Let's wait until Dr. Cossette checks her out. If she was running from someone, I don't want them to find her."

"She could've been delirious when she was saying those things."

"That's possible, but . . ." Charlie lifted one of the woman's wrists.

That's when Mateo saw the marks—marks indicating she'd been tied up.

Rose had marks just like that on her wrists and ankles when her body had been discovered.

His heart pounded harder at the similarity.

Charlie patted the pockets of the woman's dress.

"No ID. No money. No phone." Charlie sighed. "She literally ran with just the clothes on her back. It takes a lot of fear to make someone do that."

Mateo studied the woman's face for any sign of recognition. Something about her . . . he didn't know what . . . but something seemed familiar.

She appeared to be in her late twenties. She had gentle features and a petite frame. Her sundress was dirty and torn. Her bare feet were coated in dust and dotted with blisters.

She didn't have a ring on her finger to indicate she was married or engaged. But there had to be someone out there looking for her—someone besides whoever she'd escaped from. The necklace with the delicate heart pendant seemed to indicate that.

"Where do you think she came from?" Mateo finally asked.

"From the nearest road, she would've had to walk at least twenty miles," a deep voice said.

Monroe appeared in the doorway, a frown tugging at his lips.

"Did she say anything when you found her?" Monroe asked.

Her words flashed back in Mateo's mind. "She seemed to think I was going to take her back to wherever she came from. I told her I wasn't going to hurt her. That's when she said not to let them find her. Then she blacked out again."

"We'll get to the bottom of this," Monroe muttered.

Charlie let out a long breath. "Hopefully, sooner rather than later."

Mateo stared at the woman again before lifting a prayer up to his *Padre Celestial* for the woman's well-being.

His gut told him they were making the right decision by not taking her to the hospital. The wounds on her wrists and ankles spoke volumes.

She'd escaped from someone.

Someone ruthless.

Someone like the person who'd killed his wife.

———

Emily jerked her eyes open and shot up straight.

Her heart pounded.

As she glanced around the stark room, panic raced through her.

Had Arrow found her? One of his men? Had he taken her captive again?

She didn't know. All she knew was that she had to get out of here.

She swung her legs off the bed and started forward, but she was tied up again.

Her eyes jerked to her wrist.

No, not tied up.

She was hooked up to . . . an IV.

"Glad to see you're awake." A man appeared in front of her.

Emily's lungs seized at the sight of him, and she started to scramble back, to put as much distance between them as possible.

The man stepped back and held up his hands. "Hey, it's okay. You're safe here."

She stared at him, her heart still thrumming in her ears.

Safe? She didn't even know what that word meant anymore.

But she was certain she couldn't trust this man—that she couldn't trust *any* man. Kyle had preyed on her trust and taken away every ounce of her self-worth and dignity.

Never again would she let that happen.

The man had backed away, but he still stood between her and the door.

She wouldn't make it past him.

Emily remained withdrawn, confident the man could easily overpower her and all too aware that she had nothing to defend herself with. Her adrenaline might give her a burst of energy, but the man looked strong.

He also looked familiar. His dark hair. His light brown skin. His concerned brown eyes.

This was the man who'd found her in the desert.

But why did she feel like she'd seen him before?

She had no idea . . . unless he was one of Arrow's men.

Fear shot through her as her survival instincts kicked in.

She had to find a way out of here.

"My name is Mateo." His voice sounded deep and soothing. "I brought you here after I found you in the desert. You'd passed out and needed help. That's all I want to do—to help. No strings attached."

Emily released a pent-up breath. But she couldn't let down her guard.

If she died, corrupt men would continue to prey on people who desperately needed help.

She couldn't let that happen.

Mateo shifted a few steps closer. "Can you tell me your name?"

Emily remained quiet, trying to figure out if she could trust this guy. Nothing seemed certain at the moment.

"It's okay if you're not ready to talk," the man continued. "But the sooner we know who you are, the sooner we can get you back—"

"No!" Panic filled her veins and lungs at his words. "I don't . . . I don't want to . . ." She licked her dry lips. "To go . . . back there."

She'd escaped from a living nightmare.

But she couldn't go back home either—however, that was for reasons this man would probably never understand.

Her family was safer if she wasn't with them. Plus, if her parents saw her like this . . . they would be crushed. They'd already lost one daughter. She never wanted to see her mom and dad in that kind of agony again.

The man's features seemed to soften. "We'll just take this step-by-step, okay?"

The man seemed nice. Tough but gentle. Strong but understanding. Handsome but grounded.

Yet Emily knew how these people worked. None of them looked like wolves. No, initially, they all seemed like gentle, affable sheep.

Her entire body began trembling as she remembered the nightmare she'd been through.

She stared at Mateo, searching his gaze for signs of deception. "Do you . . . work for . . . Arrow?"

Mateo tilted his head, his perceptive eyes consuming her every word. "Arrow?"

Emily didn't answer for fear of saying the wrong thing.

Before the man asked any more questions, a thirty-something woman with wavy auburn hair and a white lab coat breezed into the room.

A doctor, Emily realized.

Maybe this visit would buy her more time to figure out her next plan of action . . . and if she should hide out here or try to escape.

CHAPTER 3

As the doctor examined the woman, Mateo wandered into Charlie's office.

But his mind remained on the situation. On the wounds on the woman's wrists. On the vague sense of familiarity he felt when he looked at her.

Then he remembered the haunting photo he'd been sent of Rose.

Mateo had come to this ranch to start over. To put the past behind him. To rescue women before they suffered like his wife had.

So why did he somehow feel like his past was catching up with him?

Should he tell Charlie about that photo he'd received?

Mateo frowned.

He wasn't sure yet. He liked to keep personal things private.

But what if trouble had followed him here? He wouldn't forgive himself if that was the case.

He paused in the doorway to Charlie's office and recounted to her the conversation he'd just had with their Jane Doe, careful to mention that she'd said the name "Arrow."

"The woman is definitely spooked," he concluded.

Charlie remained surprisingly quiet as she leaned back in her seat. Monroe stood beside her, acting like his normal self—quiet, brooding, intimidating.

The two were inseparable. Mateo wasn't sure if Monroe was a bodyguard, right-hand man, or romantic partner. Maybe all three. Mateo wasn't about to ask.

Charlie wasn't the type to answer personal questions. She shared what she shared when she wanted to share. Mateo could respect that.

"We don't know what she's been through," Charlie finally said. "But I'm betting that whatever happened to her was horrific—especially given the blood we found on her."

"But she had no wounds to explain the blood. You think it's someone else's?"

Charlie shrugged. "It's a possibility."

He bit back a frown. What *had* happened to her?

He spotted the map on Charlie's desk and stepped closer. "Are you trying to figure out where she came from?"

Charlie glanced at the map and sighed. "The highway makes the most sense. Otherwise, only a few people live on the perimeter of the mountains near our property. But, as you know, we monitor them. No one patrolling the area has reported any signs of anything suspicious."

"Any missing person's reports pop up?"

"Not yet. I even went back several months to see if there were any reports of someone matching this woman's description who disappeared a while ago. But there's nothing."

Mateo sighed as he rubbed his tight jaw. "She didn't appear out of thin air. So who is she?"

Charlie's gaze locked with his. "That's what we need to find out."

Mateo frowned as his thoughts raced. "We'll keep looking for answers. Maybe if this woman learns to trust us, she'll be willing to talk."

"If she stays, you mean."

They all knew she could run. That she probably would.

When you looked beyond her fear, a fighting sense of determination lingered in her gaze. There was more to this woman. She wasn't only someone who'd been victimized and escaped. There was more to her story.

What exactly was she hiding?

"Don't worry about that." Mateo placed his hands on his hips. "I won't let her get too far."

Charlie raised an eyebrow.

He shrugged. "The woman obviously needs someone to watch her back."

"I agree. Let's try to keep her here if she'll go along with it. For now, we should let her think this ranch is simply a horse rescue. We don't want the wrong person learning what we do here."

"Absolutely."

They never forced anyone to stay. Most of the women who came had been in awful situations —*abusive* situations. Recently, the team had also brought several human trafficking victims to live here as the need continued to grow.

Charlie had just signed a contract to purchase additional property adjoining the ranch. She wanted to build a lodge on it to house women who'd been victims of human trafficking. The old dude ranch just couldn't accommodate everyone who needed them.

It was a bad problem to have—bad because it was a reminder of the evil existing in the world. But

Mateo was glad to see good-hearted people working earnestly to help those in need.

This was a safe space. They were working hard to keep it that way.

That's why no one in the surrounding area knew what the ranch really did. Everyone thought it was simply a place for abused and neglected horses. But Vanishing Ranch was so, so much more.

It was a sanctuary for the hurting, for the lost, for those who'd hit dead end after dead end and now needed to start again.

Mateo tucked his hands into his pockets, his thoughts still on that photo he'd received of Rose.

He opened his mouth, about to say something, when his phone buzzed.

It was another photo.

From the same number connected with the photo of his wife.

But this time, it was a picture of the woman he'd rescued tonight.

The background was dark and indiscernible. But the camera's flash illuminated her sundress. Illuminated the bruises on her face.

In an instant, flashbacks of Mateo's wife's abduction tried to swallow him whole. He reeled back in time to the most agonizing period of his life. Grief panged with every heartbeat.

"Mateo?" Charlie stared at him.

He lowered the phone.

Then he told her about the photos he'd received.

Rose and this woman were connected . . . and he had no idea how.

But he knew with certainty that he had to find out —if it was the last thing he did.

———

Emily awoke with a start.

She'd been sleeping hard. The doctor must have given her some type of sedative to help her rest.

She sat up and gulped in several deep breaths as everything flashed back to her.

These people had rescued her . . . or had they?

The people here might seem nice . . . but so had Arrow's guys.

When she'd first awakened after being abducted, a woman had pretended to help her. Said everything would be okay. That she would take care of Emily.

In reality, the woman had been trying to get information from Emily—information about Graves into Gardens, the nonprofit Emily worked for. The organization raised millions of dollars to send to charities they sponsored throughout the world.

However, when that much money was involved, greedy people often set their sights on it.

Emily had never thought the job would put her life on the line.

But it had.

Those very people had gone through deadly lengths as they tried to force her to use her power to get them that money.

Now she didn't know who to trust. How to protect the people she loved. What the best course of action might be.

Most people in her situation would call their family. But she couldn't do that.

Besides, she was supposed to be in Mexico City right now. No one expected her back home for five more days. That should buy her some time to figure things out before anyone became concerned.

She glanced around, wondering where that man had gone—Mateo, he'd said his name was.

She didn't want to be fascinated by him, but she was.

Even though he had a haunted gaze, he still came across like a knight in shining armor. But men like that were too good to be true.

It would be better if she could avoid him—at least until she had some answers.

As if reading her thoughts, the man suddenly

appeared in her doorway, holding something in his hands.

"I thought you might be hungry," he murmured. "Dr. Cossette said she cleared you to eat."

He stepped inside with a tray laden with some soup and bread. He set it on the rolling table beside her and shifted it in front of her.

The savory scent of broth made her stomach grumble.

She stared at the man, still perplexed at how familiar he seemed.

Even though he'd rescued her out in the desert, that didn't mean Emily should trust him now. She couldn't make that mistake again.

But she *was* hungry.

She thanked him and moved the soup closer. Under his watchful eye, she took the first sip. Beef and vegetable had never tasted so good.

She hadn't eaten since she'd been abducted.

"Do you want me to get you a phone so you can call someone?" Mateo asked.

Emily's parents' faces flashed through her mind.

Now that she'd escaped, what if those guys went after them also?

Or was Emily the one they truly wanted?

The thoughts clashed in her head.

"What do you think about that phone call?" the man asked, still waiting for her answer.

She jerked her gaze back to meet Mateo's. "I . . . I don't know right now."

His shoulders rose in a brief, nonjudgmental shrug. "Okay. That's not a problem. Do you want to tell me your name yet?"

She stared at him another moment, trying to read his expression and body language. Nothing about him appeared deceitful. His gaze was steady. He didn't fidget. His pitch was even.

She supposed there would be no harm in sharing her first name. "Emily."

"It's nice to meet you, Emily."

She took another sip of soup. Every swallow seemed to stir up her hunger even more.

She grabbed the bread and took a bite, not bothering to slather any butter on it.

"Dr. Cossette said your vitals are good," Mateo continued.

"Thank you for helping me." Emily *was* grateful for his help—she only hoped his kindness wasn't a manipulation tactic.

As the man stared at her, she saw the curiosity in his gaze.

What was he thinking?

Whatever it was, he didn't push her. But it was

almost as if he had questions on his mind—questions he couldn't ask.

Probably normal in circumstances like these.

"Can I get you anything else?" he asked.

She shook her head. "I'm fine. Thank you."

Instead, he nodded and reached for the door. As he did, his sleeve pulled back, revealing a tattoo of a dove with its wings extended in flight on his forearm.

She sucked in a breath.

She'd seen that exact tattoo before.

She tried to keep her expression placid. If this man knew about the connection she'd just made, that could put her in danger. Maybe she should just play along until she could figure things out.

"Okay then," Mateo continued. "I'll be back in the morning to check on you. There's a button on the wall beside your bed. If you need anything, press it and someone will come."

Emily watched as Mateo left. She wanted to believe he had good intentions. She really did.

But she couldn't stay here.

She'd seen that same tattoo on Arrow.

CHAPTER 4

As soon as everything grew quiet and darkness fully settled on the ranch, Emily stood from her bed. She grabbed her IV line and braced herself. Counting to three, she tugged the plastic tube.

She winced as she felt a pinch and blood gushed from her skin where it had been inserted.

Queasiness churned inside her, but she had to push through it. She hated needles—almost as much as she hated snakes and darkness. But fear wouldn't stop her from escaping.

Staying here any longer than necessary was a risk she couldn't take, especially now that she believed Mateo and Arrow were working together.

She pressed some gauze against the area to stop

the bleeding then found a Band-Aid in one of the drawers and placed it over the wound.

She glanced around the room again. She thought she'd seen someone bring some clothes in earlier. Opening a closet in the corner, relief washed through her.

A stack of clothing waited there. Perfect.

Emily knew she couldn't wear the sundress she'd had on earlier. Instead, she quickly dressed in some jean shorts, a black T-shirt, and tennis shoes. A drawstring bag was also in the closet, so she grabbed that as well, knowing it could come in handy.

Emily knew firsthand how treacherous a trek through the desert could be.

This time, she wouldn't make the mistake of going into the desert without any supplies.

She slowly cracked the door open, careful not to make any noise.

She glanced up and down the dark hallway but didn't see anyone.

Then she wandered from the clinic into what appeared to be a large, cafeteria-style dining room. The scent of grilled meat and garlic still filled the air, and her stomach rumbled. The soup had been good, but it hadn't lasted long.

However, hunger was the least of her concerns right now.

She spotted a doorway in the distance and headed that way. Twisting the handle, she slipped inside.

It was an office. Just what she was looking for.

She snooped around until she found a map. She studied it a moment before deciding which direction she should head. Then she stuffed it into her pocket.

Stepping from the room, she glanced around again. Where there was a dining room, there should be a kitchen next to it.

She spotted another door in the distance and opened it. Sure enough, it was the kitchen.

She found some beef jerky, crackers, and several bottles of water and shoved them into her bag. At least it would be *something*.

She paused, fear shimmying through her at the thought of what she was about to do.

Then she remembered that dove tattoo she'd seen on Mateo.

She had no choice but to leave.

God, by Your grace, please let me get through this. Please. I can't do this on my own.

A noise across the room made her freeze.

What was that?

She sunk into the shadows, desperate not to be discovered.

The clanking sounded again.

The icemaker, Emily realized. It was only the icemaker.

She wanted to laugh with relief but couldn't.

If only that was the scariest thing she might encounter tonight.

She pulled the drawstring bag over her arms like a backpack and stepped through the kitchen exit.

Emily wasn't sure if she was up for the task before her or not.

But she definitely knew she wasn't prepared to stay here.

Her life and safety depended on getting as far away from here as possible.

———

Mateo lingered in the corner of the dining room, in the shadows where no one would see him. He wore black—which was a coincidence. He hadn't meant to, but right now the color worked in his favor.

Something in his gut told him if the woman he'd found was going to run, it would be tonight. Charlie had agreed she was a flight risk. Mateo would've sat in the hallway outside the clinic, but he knew their guest wouldn't welcome having a guard nearby.

So, he'd decided to discretely keep an eye on her.

He'd watched Emily leave the clinic and go into Charlie's office.

But why? What was she doing in there? Looking for information?

What if the woman wasn't an innocent victim as she portrayed herself? Somehow, she was connected with Rose.

What if she had something to do with his wife's death?

Then he remembered the blood he'd found on her.

If it wasn't her blood . . . then where had it come from?

Had she done something horrible to someone else?

He stored that thought in the back of his mind.

She'd left the office and wandered into the kitchen. He'd heard her rummaging for food. Had heard the icemaker grumble and heard her gasp in response.

As his mom would say, she was jumpier than a flea in a frying pan.

Right now, she stood in the doorway, still looking skittish.

Emily was clearly terrified.

He continued to watch as she stepped from the kitchen and glanced around. Then she quietly crept across the room. She reached the exit, opened the door, and stepped outside.

Moving quickly, Mateo exited through the back so he could circle the building and catch up to her without being seen.

As he reached the front, he paused near the corner and watched.

The woman walked toward the gate at the front of the property and paused.

She glanced around as if searching for other ways out.

There weren't any.

Her shoulders sank a moment before she seemed to resign herself. She began to climb.

Mateo frowned. He'd hoped she would change her mind. Realize how dangerous it was to leave this place. That she'd decide to give this ranch a chance.

She hadn't.

Mateo inched closer, staying behind a few ornamental trees and shrubs near the mess hall doors.

There weren't many places to hide on the property. It was better that way so his team could see anyone coming or going. But right now, Mateo needed to remain unseen.

If Emily managed to climb the gate, once she was on the other side there would be nothing but wide-open spaces—except for a few Joshua trees.

Mateo waited, knowing that patience was his friend in this situation. That's what Rose had always told him.

She landed on the other side of the gate with a thud, straightened, and glanced around.

She had no idea what she was getting herself into. People died out in the desert all the time. They got lost. Dehydrated.

It was too easy to get turned around.

After a moment, she began walking west.

In the very direction she'd come from.

Mateo would bet the woman didn't realize that. Even with a map, this area was hard to understand and navigate. Every direction looked the same. And she'd been so out of it when he rescued her.

He gave her a head start before departing after her. He'd give her some time in the desert before he tried to convince her to come back.

Because he had a feeling that after a few hours out there, she might wish she'd never left the ranch.

Sure, she'd been out there in the desert earlier. But now, it was dark.

And the desert at night held entirely different challenges.

CHAPTER 5

Fear rushed through Emily as she stared at the vast emptiness of the land around her.

Her only comfort at the moment was the sprinkling of stars above. What appeared to be the Milky Way rose over the mountains.

The stars didn't help her see much through the darkness, but she hadn't even looked for a flashlight. She couldn't risk broadcasting her location to anyone who might be watching.

She'd managed to escape from Arrow once.

What if she wasn't so lucky this time? What if Arrow or one of his men found her? What if Mateo truly did work with Arrow and he came after her? He might not be as nice this time. His true colors might emerge.

She shivered at the thought and at the cold air.

The temperatures had dropped since earlier. She should have hunted around for a sweatshirt or jacket.

Instead, she rubbed the goosebumps rising across her skin.

Something about the desert had always both fascinated and terrified her.

Right now, terror had a tight grip on her. It tried to control her. To paralyze her.

She couldn't let fear win.

Emily didn't know where she was going or what she would do when she got there.

Were the police a safe option? Or were they in on the whole operation?

She didn't know.

But if she didn't return home to LA, where would she go?

She had no car and no money.

She couldn't even catch a train or a bus.

If she could find a phone, she could call the FBI. That would be the smart thing to do, she supposed. But she feared what the pushback would be. What these guys might do to the people she cared about once they realized she'd turned them in.

The thoughts all collided in her head.

Despair threatened to sink into her again, but Emily fought it. She had to be stronger than that if she was going to survive this ordeal.

She remembered going to Sedona with some of her friends while in college. They'd set out on a hike without first properly doing their research. What they'd assumed would be an hour or two hike had ended up taking eight hours.

At times they hadn't been sure they'd find their way out of the wilderness. Their feet had been sore and blistered. Their muscles tight and tired. Their hope had been waning.

Eventually, they'd reached civilization again.

It would be that way now also . . . Emily hoped.

Please, Lord. I don't know what I'm doing. But if I stay and hide, innocent people will suffer. I have the power to stop it. Am I strong enough? Plus, if I stayed . . . it could be dangerous. What if that man works for Arrow? They have the same tattoo. I can't ignore that.

But with every step, her fear and despair grew stronger and more overpowering.

She gripped the straps of her backpack like lifelines.

She just needed to be careful.

But as her foot landed on a loose rock, she lunged forward.

She hit the ground, and something sharp dug into her skin. Tears immediately pricked her eyes.

Turning, she grabbed her bicep and saw the small needles there.

She'd landed on some kind of cactus, she realized.

Great. Another obstacle she didn't need.

Sitting up, she winced as she tried to pull out a needle embedded into her skin.

There must be twenty.

Her tears quickly became sobs. Not because of the cactus.

But because of . . . everything.

There was no way she would survive this escape. She should have known better.

No matter how she looked at the situation, she wouldn't win.

Just then, a footfall sounded behind her.

Fear shot up her spine.

They'd found her, hadn't they?

————

"I know I'm probably the last person you want to see." Mateo stepped in front of Emily, careful not to make any sudden moves and spook her further.

He'd been following her, and she'd been clueless.

It wasn't a good sign. Sure, he could be quiet and stealthy.

But still, what if it hadn't been *him* following her?

Mateo had seen her tumble. Seen her hit that cactus.

Heard her sobs afterward.

That's when he knew he had to step in.

However, the more he thought about those pictures that had been sent to him, the more curious he was about the ranch's newest guest.

What if she'd been sent to VR as a decoy? As a mole?

Because he saw someone extremely capable behind those dark eyes of hers. She wasn't someone who'd lived in the margins and who'd been victimized.

No, she knew more than she was admitting. The blood he'd seen on her dress seemed to confirm that.

He wasn't going to be able to force that information from her, however.

Emily scrambled away, crab-crawling as she fought to put distance between them. To escape.

If she wasn't careful, she'd run into another cactus —or even worse, a snake. More than one variety of rattlesnake called this area home.

"I'm not going to hurt you." Mateo sensed her overwhelming fear and knelt beside her, hoping to seem less imposing. "I know you have no reason to believe me or to trust me. I don't know what you've been through, and I can't begin to understand. But I don't want to see you die out here."

When she said nothing, he continued.

"Dying in the desert is no way to go. You can only live three days without water—less out here in this heat. Then you'll begin to get delirious. Your vision will become blurry. The good news is that you'll most likely pass out before you die."

"What do you want from me?" Her voice cracked as she stared up at him.

"Let me take you back to the ranch. We'll get you healthy. Then you can figure out what you want to do. If you want to stay or if you want to go. If you want to call someone or if you just want to disappear off the face of the earth. It's not my choice. It's yours. I won't force you to stay. I won't force you to do anything."

If she chose to return, Mateo would be keeping a close eye on her, but she didn't need to know that.

She stared at him another moment, almost as if she were still trying to figure out whether or not she could believe him. Her eyes were wide. Her breathing shallow. Her limbs trembling.

One thing was for sure: her fear was real, even if her motives were questionable.

Mateo rose and rested his hands on his hips. He hadn't expected to use his negotiating skills since he'd resigned from the Mexican federal police. But old habits were hard to break.

"We can help you," he finally said.

"I've heard that before. Promises that were lies meant to manipulate me." The woman's voice cracked.

"We're not going to do that to you." Mateo stared at her as he waited for her response. "You know, trust goes both ways. We really don't know much about you either."

Her eyes widened even more, as if she hadn't considered the possibility he might not believe everything she'd told him.

Before she responded, something in the distance caught his eye.

A light.

Not just one light. *Three* lights.

Based on the movement, the beams came from flashlights.

If he had to guess, whoever held those flashlights were at the base of the mountain range.

That meant someone—or three someones—were too close for his comfort.

The woman followed his gaze and sucked in a sharp breath. "Are those your guys?"

"No, they're not."

Quickly, she stood, her chin trembling. "Please, don't let them find me. They'll kill me if they do."

At once, images of Rose filled Mateo's mind.

Memories of the pictures her captors had sent him. Memories of her suffering.

Mateo had felt so helpless. He hadn't been able to stop the men from harming her. Hadn't been able to stop them from taking her life.

Mateo may not have been able to save Rose, but he wouldn't allow himself to ever fail someone who was depending on him . . . not again.

Right now, he needed to figure out if this woman he'd rescued was a friend or a foe.

CHAPTER 6

Emily hoped she didn't regret trusting Mateo.

But as soon as she'd seen those lights in the distance, thoughts of Arrow had filled her mind and caused terror to race through her.

What if those were his guys?

He'd told her that if she ran, he would find her. That he'd always find her. That he would do everything within his power to get what he wanted from her.

Arrow seemed like the type of guy who did what he promised—especially when his promises were deadly.

Emily stepped closer to Mateo, a new desperation capturing her trembling muscles.

Then his tattoo slammed back into her mind, and another round of panic washed through her.

She eyed him. "Who are you really? Because if you're going to kill me, just do it. Get it over with."

"I'm not going to kill you."

She nodded at his arm. "You work for him, don't you?"

He glanced down and touched his tattoo before looking back at her, his eyes narrowed. "You think I work for this Arrow guy?"

"Don't treat me like an idiot. You both have the same tattoo." The words came out through gritted teeth.

Surprise washed through his gaze, and he glanced down at his arm again. "Several of the guys I went through the academy with have this same tattoo."

She stared at him. "The academy?"

"I was a federal police officer in Mexico."

Her head swirled, and she took a step back.

If that was the case, then Arrow probably had more powerful connections than she'd ever imagined.

She took another step away.

He raised his hand. "Don't run. Please. I promise I won't hurt you."

She glanced back and saw the flashlights getting brighter—closer.

Then she glanced at Mateo again.

Could she really trust this man?

The wrong choice would get her killed. She was certain of it.

What she wasn't certain about was which choice would be correct.

"I'll go with you," she finally said. "But please don't make me regret this."

"I won't." He nodded at her bicep. "Do you need me to take those needles out?"

"No, I'd rather get away from these guys first." She took a step toward him, not seeing the rock beneath her.

She stumbled forward—and right into Mateo.

She gasped as she hit his solid chest. His hands grasped her—avoiding the cactus needles—as he held her up.

The breath left her lungs at their closeness.

Slowly, she pulled her gaze up to meet his. Her heart seemed to sputter as she looked into his brown eyes. His hard jaw. His full lips.

As a rush of attraction swept through her, she pushed back. "Sorry."

"You have to watch your step out here." He pointed at the rocks spread across the ground.

She resisted a scowl. His words were true. She was just annoyed—mostly at herself.

Mateo's gaze held hers, something almost mysterious lingering there—like he knew something she didn't. "Is it okay if I hold your uninjured arm as we walk?"

He was asking her? It seemed like such a gentlemanly thing to do. But she had to be careful not to let his charms win her over. And she *really* needed to forget just how strong he'd felt when she'd stumbled into his arms.

She nodded. "Okay."

Back in LA, Emily hadn't dated a lot. She'd been busy with her career and her friends. The men she had dated were few and far between, and they seemed harmless. Benign. Almost boring.

Until Kyle. He'd been too good to be true—because he was. It had all been an act.

After Kyle had betrayed her . . . everything had changed.

Emily learned not every kind gesture was sincere.

But Mateo somehow seemed different.

Then she remembered his tattoo again.

What sense did it make? Had he told her the truth about the academy?

Mateo held her elbow, just as he'd said. He didn't try to pull her close. Didn't try to manhandle her.

Instead, Mateo ushered her away from those lights and toward the ranch. As they walked, he pulled out his phone and made a call, muttering something to the person on the other line. It sounded like he was informing someone at the ranch that they were returning.

As Emily glanced in the distance, she couldn't even see the ranch anymore. She knew it wasn't because she'd walked that far.

With everyone asleep, the place was dark except for a few exterior lights. If someone didn't know the dwelling existed, they probably wouldn't even notice the property.

Mateo kept hold of her elbow as he watched their surroundings.

On occasion, he glanced back, probably searching for those lights.

A shiver raced through Emily at the realization.

She couldn't bear to look for herself. Couldn't bear the realization that Arrow's men might still be out there. That they might be searching for her. Closing in, even.

Finally, they made it to the ranch.

Mateo punched in numbers at the keypad on the gate and then led her inside.

A woman waited for them near the entrance— Charlie, if Emily remembered correctly. She vaguely remembered the woman talking to her in the clinic, but everything was fuzzy.

The woman had straight, dark hair, striking features, and intelligent green eyes. She wore jeans tight enough to show her shapely legs and an equally fitted top.

"You're in good hands now." Mateo led her toward Charlie. "Charlie will take care of you. I need to go back out there for a while."

Emily nodded, hoping gratitude shone in her gaze. She couldn't bring herself to say the words *thank you*. She didn't know why. It didn't make sense.

But it was probably because she still didn't know if she could trust him. The uncertainty made her feel jumpy, made her chest tight.

"We're going to get you all taken care of." Charlie's voice sounded confident but compassionate. "Mateo, take someone with you when you go back out."

"Yes, ma'am." He nodded and took off toward the stable.

Charlie led her back toward the clinic. Emily couldn't help but wonder what this woman's story was. Based on her commanding voice, she seemed to be in charge.

Before slipping inside the building, Emily took

one last glance back at Mateo as he and a woman rode their horses toward the gate.

She only wished she knew who she could truly trust.

She shivered again as she realized she'd never felt so alone.

———

Mateo and Ainsley Tatum rode in the direction of those lights.

Ainsley had only been at the ranch for a month. She was a former rodeo girl turned Texas Ranger. But she'd left her law enforcement position to come here.

He wondered what her story was.

It seemed as if everyone who came to work at Vanishing Ranch had a story. They had their own motives for wanting to help, their own past that led them to this place in life.

Right now, Mateo focused on the landscape in front of him. He couldn't afford a misstep.

But his thoughts continually went back to Emily's comment. He had the same tattoo as this Arrow guy? How was that even possible?

Twelve people who'd gone through the academy with him had gotten matching tattoos, just like he said. He kept in touch with many of those men.

He couldn't see any of them abducting a woman and beating her.

Besides, what was the connection between this woman and Rose?

He wanted to ask her—but the timing wasn't right yet.

He needed to bring this up on his terms.

"You see lights out here a lot?" Ainsley's voice pulled him from his thoughts.

"Never. It makes me wonder what's going on."

"Definitely. The desert has its own personality, doesn't it?"

"Absolutely. The desert is where you go to find yourself. That's what my dad always said."

"Sounds about right."

Mateo surveyed the area in front of them. If danger was closing in, he needed to stop it.

Finally, he and Ainsley reached the area where he'd seen the lights.

"No one's here." Ainsley glanced around. "They're gone."

Suspicion tightened his spine. This was the same spot he'd seen those vultures circling earlier. "Are they?"

What if they weren't gone? What if the people with the flashlights were hiding? In a situation like this, he and Ainsley had to proceed with the utmost caution.

Mateo took a flashlight from his waist and shone it on the ground.

Sure enough, the foliage was disturbed.

Footprints circled the area.

Someone had definitely been here.

He slid off his horse and bent closer for a better look.

A rectangular indentation marred the ground, the edges of it appearing curved, as if created with a shovel.

More memories of Rose's death hit him again.

Someone had also sent him pictures back then, back when she'd been abducted.

Pictures of her makeshift grave. First, of it being dug. Then of an empty hole in the dry ground. Then with dirt scattered over Rose's lifeless body.

His throat tightened with emotion at the reminder of her senseless death.

Those pictures. His tattoo. Emily's sudden appearance. They were all somehow connected. But how?

Unease churned inside him.

Using his boot, he kicked some dirt aside.

The normally packed soil was definitely loose.

He kicked away more dirt and kept doing so until his boot hit something.

Ainsley shone her flashlight on the area and gasped.

A face stared back at them.

A pale, lifeless face.

CHAPTER 7

Emily stared at the woman beside her as they stepped into the main building. She fully expected Charlie to lead her through the cafeteria and back into the small clinic.

Instead, the woman said, "Let's get you to my office. I'll help you remove those cactus needles there."

They went to the same office where Emily had grabbed the map. She thought about saying something to Charlie about it and returning the map, but she quickly decided not to mention it. Instead, she'd keep it and familiarize herself with the area a little more.

Charlie directed Emily to sit in a chair. As she did, Charlie grabbed something from her drawer—a first aid kit—and opened it. She pulled out some tweezers and then sat in front of her.

"This might sting a little," she murmured.

Emily squeezed her eyes shut as a prickly needle jerked from her skin.

Charlie was right. The needles stung.

"I just want you to know this ranch is a safe place." Charlie paused and locked gazes with her. "We don't keep people here against their wills. But we don't let them walk into danger either. I like to think of this ranch as a sanctuary, a place where people can heal."

Emily listened.

"Healing isn't always easy. In fact, it's downright painful sometimes. It's scary. It feels uncertain. But if you give us some time, we'll help you through each phase of that process." Charlie paused again. "Think about it, okay?"

Emily nodded.

The way Charlie described this ranch . . . it almost seemed too good to be true. And if something seemed too good to be true? It probably was.

Kyle was the perfect example.

"I'm glad you're back with us." Charlie plucked another needle out. "Dr. Cossette says you were dehydrated and have some cuts and bruises. Otherwise, you're okay. How would you like to stay in a cabana tonight instead of in the clinic? You seem to be walking just fine on your own so I think that will be okay."

"A cabana?" Curiosity lilted in her voice.

Charlie smiled, the expression soothing and friendly. "That's what the previous owner of this place called them—it used to be a dude ranch. I'm considering calling them guesthouses instead. Seems more fitting, right?"

Emily's thoughts continued to race. Was this her answer to prayer? A safe space where she could recalculate the future?

She dragged her gaze back up to meet Charlie's as she contemplated that question. "Who would I be staying with?"

"By yourself. It's just a bedroom and a bathroom, but I think you'll find it sufficient and comfortable." Charlie stared at her another moment, her gaze searching Emily's eyes. "Would you like that?"

Emily didn't have to think long before she nodded. "Yes, I would."

"Great. Any more questions?"

She had a million. But she settled on, "How trustworthy is Mateo?"

Charlie didn't hesitate. "I wouldn't have brought him here if I didn't trust him. He's a good guy. Skilled. Operates with integrity."

She sounded so certain.

Emily wished she could believe her.

But between the remote location of this place, Mateo's tattoo, and the secrets behind his gaze, something didn't add up.

Emily needed to figure out what.

Charlie's phone beeped, and she answered. Her expression quickly turned grim, and she stood.

"You'll have to excuse me," she muttered. "I have a situation I need to take care of."

Alarm raced through Emily. "Is everything okay?"

"Mateo found a dead body."

———

Mateo saw the lights of the UTV coming his way, and he flagged it down.

A moment later, Charlie and Monroe climbed from the vehicle and joined them.

"You found a body?" Charlie raised an eyebrow.

He nodded toward the makeshift grave. "Right over here."

Ever since he'd found the body, all he'd been able to think about was the blood on Emily. About the fact she'd been out here earlier. That she didn't have any answers for them.

What if she'd killed this man and then buried him? What if those people with the flashlights had been out here searching for this missing person?

Emily's presence here could be more involved than she was letting on.

He hated to be so jaded, but he just didn't know if he could trust the woman yet.

"Did they leave any tracks?" Monroe asked. "Can we follow them?"

"Ainsley already tried," Mateo said. "They headed toward the mountains, but then the tracks disappeared as if they'd swept them away."

Charlie peered at the dead man's face, shining her light on him. "I don't recognize him. You?"

Mateo shook his head. "I'm guessing he's in his twenties. His neat haircut indicates maybe he worked an office job. Could have even been military."

Charlie grunted as she stared at the man's face.

"What do you want us to do?" Ainsley stood from where she'd been observing the body and wiped the dusty dirt from her knees. "Call the police?"

Charlie's gaze darkened. "They're probably going to want to check out the ranch if we do that. Ask people questions. We're the closest residents. I don't want to traumatize any of our guests, however."

"It's your call," Mateo said.

"We can't *not* report this body," Monroe reminded Charlie.

When he spoke, it was usually because he had something important to say.

Charlie let out a long breath. "I know. I just don't like the trouble this could bring with it. Our newest resident could have a connection to this."

Those were Mateo's thoughts also, but he didn't say that out loud.

"I'll call the sheriff," Charlie finally said. "You and Ainsley head back to the ranch and let the others know what's happening. While Monroe and I are waiting here, we'll snap some pictures of this guy, just in case he's connected with Emily. Got it?"

"Yes, ma'am," Mateo muttered.

"I'm not going to mention the woman to the cops. I'm not saying we can't trust law enforcement around here, but she doesn't want anyone to know she's here. I'd like to respect her wishes—at least until we know more details."

"Understood."

He glanced at the man's body again.

The bad feeling in his gut continued to grow.

Was this man connected in some way with Emily?

It seemed too much of a coincidence to think otherwise.

CHAPTER 8

Emily woke up the next morning still feeling uneasy.

Something had happened here at the ranch last night. She'd heard voices outside. Had wondered if someone here had called the cops and told them she was here.

But no one had come to her cabana.

Still, her curiosity burned inside.

When she opened the door, a cardboard box with her name on it was waiting there. She brought it inside and found some more new clothes as well as some toiletry items. A note on top said: **Come to breakfast whenever you're ready. ~ Charlie**

Some of Emily's anxiety eased. She had food and clothes. Her own private space.

She had the freedom to enter and leave her cabana as she pleased.

Maybe this ranch wasn't as bad as she'd assumed. Still, she couldn't be too quick to trust.

Emily quickly showered, the water refreshing as it washed over her. But as she ran the washcloth over her body, she paused near the marks on her wrists and ankles. She even had a few bruises she hadn't noticed before.

Flashbacks of her abduction hit her, and she pressed her eyes closed.

She'd never felt so helpless. So desperate. Almost as if she'd do anything if it meant getting out of the dungeon where she'd been held captive for nearly two days.

She'd never experienced feelings of fear like that before.

And she never wanted to experience them again.

Anxiety squeezed her windpipe at the memories.

Flashbacks hit her—recollections of the struggle for her life she'd endured.

One that had ended with blood all over her.

She'd never forget the sight of the red all over her clothes. Never forget the smell of it.

The look in the man's eyes.

She took a few deep breaths, trying to get her thoughts under control.

As soon as she was dressed and ready, her stomach rumbled, indicating it was time for breakfast.

When she stepped outside, Mateo was waiting for her, leaning against one of the posts on the front porch of the cabana.

"*Buenos días*," he muttered.

"Good morning."

Her heart sped at the sight of him with his still-wet hair, bootcut jeans, black T-shirt, and cowboy boots.

As a breeze blew over them, the scent of Ivory soap wafted her way, speeding her heart even more.

The reaction was only because she hadn't expected to see him there.

Or maybe it was just a hero complex, Emily reminded herself. A natural reaction after someone saved your life.

He was handsome . . . and also somehow linked with her abductor.

Her throat tightened at the reminder.

Her head pounded. She didn't know what to think. Part of her wanted to trust him. But she couldn't afford to blindly believe someone, especially not when the stakes were so high.

"I've already eaten, but I thought I'd walk you to breakfast." He casually rested his hands in the pockets of his jeans. He sounded matter-of-fact . . . and not exactly warm.

He was weary of her, wasn't he?

She couldn't blame him. Not really.

Maybe it was better this way.

Emily swallowed, feeling her muscles loosen slightly. "Okay."

They walked at a slow pace beside each other toward the large building amongst the cluster of smaller structures at the ranch.

"Is everything okay?" she finally asked when he offered no information. "I noticed some commotion last night."

"I think Charlie told you this already, but . . . we found a body in the desert last night." He paused and pulled out his phone. "The picture is gruesome to look at. I apologize in advance."

He showed her his screen.

Emily forced herself to remain calm as she looked at the lifeless face staring back at her.

"Is this man familiar?" Mateo observed her as she looked at the photo.

She studied the man's face a moment before shaking her head. "I . . . I don't think so. Who is he?"

"The sheriff is trying to identify him."

"Wow . . . that's terrible. Where did you find him?"

Mateo studied her another moment, a touch of reservation—and suspicion—in his gaze. "Near where we saw the people with the flashlights."

Emily's face paled. "You think they—"

"I'm not making any assumptions. I just had to ask if you'd seen him before."

"Of course." She rubbed her throat.

Did he think she had something to do with this dead man?

She didn't. But she resisted the urge to defend herself. Doing so would only make her look guilty at this point.

Mateo walked her the rest of the way to the mess hall. "Listen, I have a meeting to go to now. But we need to talk later. Okay?"

Her eyes widened. What did he want to talk to her about?

Reluctantly, she nodded. "Okay."

"Perfect. Get yourself some breakfast, and I'll find you later."

Part of her wanted to trust this man. But she had to be smart about these things.

Especially since he seemed oddly familiar, and that tattoo . . .

That realization still left her feeling uneasy.

———

Mateo stopped by Charlie's cottage—as she'd instructed in an earlier text—and knocked on the door.

She called, "Come in!" and he opened the door.

Monroe sat on the couch close beside her, as if they'd been having a private conversation while drinking coffee. When Mateo stepped inside, they both straightened and glanced at him.

"Am I interrupting something?" Mateo raised an eyebrow.

"Not at all." Charlie crossed her arms as she looked at him, moving away from Monroe just slightly. "Have a seat."

"How did everything go last night?" he asked.

"The sheriff came and asked me questions," Charlie said. "I didn't mention to them that you'd been the one who found the body, and they didn't push to come in and talk to anyone here."

"Did they identify the body?" he continued.

"Not that I know of." Charlie shifted as her gaze narrowed. "You think Emily killed that guy?"

Mateo appreciated Charlie's tendency to get right to the point. "Gut instinct? No. But there's a lot of weird stuff happening around here."

"Agreed."

He hesitated, not really wanting to talk about Rose. But it appeared he had no other choice.

He raked a hand through his hair before starting. "Rose's captors . . . before they killed her . . . they sent me pictures of her grave. They'd dug it in advance. It was shallow. In the desert."

Charlie's eyes widened. "Another connection . . . I know this must be difficult for you and bringing up a lot of bad memories. I'm sorry."

He nodded to acknowledge her statement. "And there's this." He pointed to the tattoo of a dove on his forearm and then explained what Emily had told him. He also told Charlie the story behind his tattoo.

Charlie's eyes widened. "That's . . . weird. Do you have any idea how your tattoo could be connected?"

He rubbed his jaw. "No. But I don't like this. I'm not even sure if we can trust her, to be honest."

"You think she might be hiding something?" Charlie waited for his answer.

"I do. I think she knows more than she's telling us. We don't know where she came from. We assume she walked a long distance. But we don't know for sure. This could be a setup. She could be here to gather information. The men who killed Rose . . . they could have sent Emily here to get inside the ranch to taunt me."

"I thought her killers were either dead or behind bars."

"I shot Miguel Sanchez myself. The men who

worked with him are behind bars. But Miguel had a whole network of people. I'm sure he still has guys out there."

Charlie's frown grew deeper with every new detail. "The timing is suspicious. We don't get that many people coming out this way. We're going to need to keep an eye on the situation."

Mateo nodded, feeling the exact same way.

Who was this woman? What was their connection?

He knew one thing—he had to get to the bottom of it.

If the same people who'd killed his wife were back in his life trying to taunt him, he needed to know.

"I can sense danger closing in." The instinct had been honed from Mateo's years in law enforcement. "Something—either out in the desert or surrounding this woman I found—is off."

Charlie frowned again before glancing at Monroe. "Monroe and I were just saying the same thing. We need to figure out the connection between this woman and you."

His jaw tightened. "Exactly what I was thinking too. I'll get started on it now."

"One more thing before you go." Charlie grabbed a bag from the table and handed it to him. "Jesse found this on the fence this morning. Any idea where it came from?"

Mateo held the clear plastic bag up to the light and saw the ring inside.

He sucked in a breath as he observed the princess-cut diamond. The white-gold band. The two small diamonds on each side of the larger one.

His chest squeezed tight.

"Mateo?"

He snapped out of his daze as he turned back to Charlie. "This was Rose's. It wasn't on her finger when we found her. Now someone left it here."

CHAPTER 9

As the day continued, Emily still wasn't sure how she felt about being at the ranch.

Part of her still wanted to leave. She wanted to figure out where the men who had abducted her were hiding. Then she wanted to bring them down.

But she couldn't do that without resources—resources she didn't have right now.

Plus, her abductors had pressed her between a proverbial rock and a hard place.

Nothing seemed as simple as it once had.

If she had to choose, she'd let her life go to ruin in order to stop corrupt men.

But she couldn't be hasty about how she let that happen.

One wrong move would leave her dead and the corruption continuing.

Dr. Cossette had stopped by to check on her. The doctor said Emily was making good progress and her wounds were healing.

Unable to sit still, Emily had volunteered to help in the kitchen. She'd been given a few tasks to do throughout the day.

But she felt distracted. Too much was on her mind. Too many decisions to make.

Stay or go?

Trust or run?

Was she being selfish by staying here? Should she call the FBI?

She wasn't sure of any of those answers.

When Emily finished helping clean up after a dinner of roast beef and mashed potatoes, she took off her apron and hung it behind the door.

She glanced at Chef, a man in his late forties with dark skin, a bright smile, and a bald head. He was jovial and seemed to truly enjoy his job. She'd heard he'd worked as a chef on an aircraft carrier until he retired from the military a few years ago.

"Anything else I can do for you, Chef?"

He threw a dish towel over his shoulder and gave her a pointed look. "You've already been a huge help.

You didn't have to volunteer in the kitchen at all, you know."

Emily shrugged. "I don't mind."

He winked. "Well, thank you for all your help, Miss Emily."

She smiled. She'd actually enjoyed working for the man today.

As she began to leave, she sensed someone in the doorway.

She froze before slowly turning.

She released her breath when she saw Mateo standing there. She'd thought she would see him more today, but she hadn't. That left her wondering what he'd been doing—and what exactly he wanted to talk about.

"Didn't mean to scare you," he muttered.

She looked away, hating how attracted she felt to the man. "It's okay."

Her throat tightened at his nearness. She'd always thought she was drawn to the businessman type of guy. And Mateo was definitely *not* a businessman. He was a police officer turned cowboy.

So why did she find him so incredibly attractive? She couldn't allow herself to be blinded by illusions of romance or knights in shining armor.

Especially if this man was somehow connected with Arrow.

If anything, she needed to keep Mateo at arm's length.

"You trying to earn your keep?" He nodded toward the kitchen beyond her. He didn't sound especially friendly but almost cautious instead.

"Something like that." Emily shrugged. "Trying to keep my mind off things, and I don't like owing people anything."

"All we ask at the ranch is that you follow our rules and are honest with us."

She sensed there was something significant behind his words. She remembered the last thing he'd said to her: We need to talk later.

She'd been thinking about his words all day.

Was that why Mateo was here now?

She crossed her arms as she looked up at him. "Something on your mind?"

An unreadable emotion flickered in his gaze. "Want to take a walk?"

This was it.

The moment of truth. The talk. Her chance to find some answers.

Emily drew in a deep breath and nodded. "Sure."

She hoped she didn't regret this.

"Great. Let me show you the stable then."

She knew there was much more to this "walk" than showing her the stable.

But she would make the most of it.

Emily had always loved horses.

She didn't have much experience around them. She'd been a city girl, and her parents had always been so focused on their jobs that there wasn't time for much else. But up until she'd turned eighteen, Emily had asked for a pony every year for Christmas. It had become a running joke in her family.

As she walked outside, she reminded herself of the stakes in this situation.

She might be able to escape for a while . . . but it was only a matter of time before trouble found her again.

She couldn't stay at the ranch forever.

Soon, she was going to have to figure out her next step . . . but first, she had to figure out who she could trust.

————

Mateo needed to get information from Emily. He needed to know about her connection to Rose. Needed to know why Rose's ring had suddenly appeared here at the ranch. Needed to know how someone knew he was at the ranch.

He'd checked the security camera footage.

Nothing showed there.

The ring had been left in a small blind spot, in the no man's land of security footage—a problem Charlie was already working to fix.

But he realized that someone on the inside could have left that ring.

Had it been Emily?

He hoped this walk would do the trick.

He paused inside the stable and rubbed his stallion's nose. "This is my horse, The Lone Ranger."

The horse let out a neigh, and Mateo grabbed a treat from his pocket for him.

"He's beautiful," Emily muttered as she stared into the horse's eyes.

"I think so."

"How did he get his name?"

"Growing up, my uncle introduced me to *The Lone Ranger* TV show. I was hooked. I spent all my free time pretending I was the Lone Ranger after that —much to my parents' chagrin." He shrugged. "I guess the name just seemed appropriate."

"Makes sense to me." She paced down the stalls, and Mateo introduced her to each horse.

Near one of the last stalls, she paused in front of a brown mare, a thoroughbred. "And who's this?"

"This is Bianca."

"Bianca? All the other horses have such fancy, whimsical names. It makes hers seem ordinary."

"Bianca is the name this one came to us with, so we kept it."

Emily studied the horse's face. "What's her story?"

"She was a racehorse who stopped winning. Her owner was going to have her slaughtered. That's when Charlie rescued her. She realized there was more value to Bianca than what the horse offered on the racetrack."

"I'm glad Charlie stepped in. She's beautiful."

"She is, isn't she?" Mateo ran his hand over the horse's mane.

Bianca let out a soft neigh.

So many times, these horses came here to heal. But these animals also helped their guests to heal. An innate connection existed between humans and horses. Mateo had seen beautiful things happen between them.

The creatures had even helped him with his own healing after Rose's death.

"You sound like you know a lot about horses." Emily's voice pulled him from his thoughts.

"I grew up on a horse farm in Mexico. Horses were my life and defined a good portion of my childhood."

She glanced at him as if his words had taken her by surprise. "That sounds . . . nice."

Mateo had a great childhood, one he couldn't complain about. His parents had instilled a good work ethic in him, taught him about integrity, and provided well for him and his siblings.

She turned to him, studied him a moment, and then crossed her arms. "I know you're beating around the bush. What is it you'd really like to talk about?"

His eyebrows flickered up.

At least, she was being direct.

And she was right. He wanted to talk about something else entirely.

He was usually a "take the bull by the horns" kind of guy. But he was trying to temper himself. To be patient.

If he approached this wrong, this woman could go running again, and that wasn't what he wanted.

But he prayed he'd have the right words—kind if she needed compassion or firm if she was being deceitful.

CHAPTER 10

Emily stared at Mateo, ready to get down to business.

At least, down to business on her terms. She still wasn't ready to share too much. But they'd never find answers if they both kept secrets.

Mateo eyed her, his muscles hardening. "Who are you really?"

She swallowed hard as she contemplated how to answer. "I'm someone who was abducted three days ago. But I escaped. Then you found me."

It was the CliffsNotes version of her story, but she wasn't ready to share too many details.

His gaze remained narrow and skeptical. "Why did you sneak into Charlie's office last night?"

Her eyes widened. Of course, Mateo had seen her go in there.

She should have known.

"I wasn't trying to sneak. I was looking for a map." She tilted her head. "Did you think I was snooping?"

"I don't know what to think about you."

"I could say the same for you. Sometimes you seem compassionate. Other times, you act suspicious of me."

"Clearly trust has to be earned." His jaw flexed as their eyes met in a stare-off.

"Okay then. Trust goes both ways. Why do you have that tattoo?" She nodded to the mark on his forearm. It was all she'd been able to think about today. "I need to know more than what you told me last night."

"Like I said, my buddies and I at the academy all got them."

Nausea pooled in her stomach. He hadn't denied anything or tried to make excuses. "So you know Arrow?"

His gaze softened just slightly. "I have no idea who Arrow is. I was hoping you might offer me more information so I could figure that out."

She remained silent a moment.

"What about the blood on your dress?" he asked. "It wasn't yours."

Her nausea grew stronger, and she placed a hand

over her stomach, praying she didn't throw up as memories pummeled her. "One of the guys untied me. He had a knife and was telling me exactly what he wanted to do with me. When he touched my shoulder, I fought back. I accidentally made him slice his arm. He was furious with me."

"What happened?"

"He roughed me up pretty bad while he was still bleeding. It got all over me. Then he tied me back up to go tend to his wound, and shortly after that I was able to escape. But I didn't purposefully hurt anyone. Although . . . there was part of me that wondered if I could have killed him if I had the chance."

She hadn't meant to say the words aloud.

But they were true.

She'd been desperate. Desperation could show different sides of people, sides they didn't know they had.

Silence stretched another moment.

Her muscles remained hardened with doubt. "I can't help but wonder if you're all in on this. If I walked into a trap. If all this kindness is just an act."

He crossed his muscular arms over his chest as he stared at her. "If that's true, then why haven't you called the FBI? I offered to let you use a phone."

"I . . . I have to figure things out before I decide

what to do." Emily's voice cracked as she said the words.

"We could help, you know."

"Maybe . . . if I can trust you."

Mateo let out a frustrated breath. "Listen . . . we're not getting anywhere right now. We won't until we trust each other."

"Agreed." Her voice cracked. "But last time I trusted the wrong person, I almost died."

Mateo stared at Emily, so many questions still on his mind.

How was he going to get through to her?

Was she telling the truth? Had she just been looking for a map in Charlie's office?

Or did she have ulterior motives for being here? Was she trying to find out information about what they were doing at the ranch? They'd made a lot of people mad—wealthy men whose wives had disappeared. Politicians. Business leaders.

They had their fair share of enemies that they needed to guard against in order to continue their work at Vanishing Ranch.

Emily stared back at him. "What are we going to do?"

"Fill in the gaps. We need to find a connection in all this."

She raked her hands through her curly hair, leaving several strands tangled on top of her head. "You said you were with the Mexican federal police? I've actually worked with the federales—as Americans like to call them—before."

Mateo's eyebrows shot up. Was *that* why she was familiar?

He couldn't imagine why this woman would have worked with the Mexican federal police, though. She was clearly American.

"Is that right?" he finally said, still feeling cautious. "Tell me more."

Emily pressed her lips together before answering. "I work for a nonprofit organization that raises money for various ministries throughout the world. My job is to go in and make sure funds are being managed properly and that money is going to the people it's intended for."

"Instead of administrators padding their own pockets," Mateo finished.

"Exactly. I discovered corruption within one of the organizations we work with in Mexico. I had proof, so I reported what was happening to Mexican authorities."

His heart pounded harder as realizations settled

in his mind. "Rose worked for a ministry that helped feed local children . . ."

Emily's eyes widened. "Rose?"

"My wife."

Emily went completely still. "Wait . . . did she work for Misión de Comida?"

"She did. You're familiar with it?" His heart thrummed as he waited for Emily's response.

"Very . . ." Emily shook her head before pinching the skin between her eyes. "In fact . . . I think . . . I think I knew your wife."

As facts collided in his mind, Mateo's world seemed to stop.

CHAPTER 11

Emily stepped back until she hit one of the stable's rough walls. She leaned against it to steady herself as revelation after revelation rolled over her.

She couldn't believe this.

Rose? This was *Rose's* Mateo?

No wonder the man looked familiar.

Emily had seen pictures of him before—pictures of him with Rose. The woman had talked about him nonstop. About how much she loved him. About how great he was. About how he was the man of her dreams.

The two had been totally and completely in love.

Mateo stepped closer, his gaze now more intense. "Emily . . . I need to know more."

His voice didn't leave any room for argument. Instead, his hard-set gaze almost looked demanding.

But she could understand, given the situation.

Still . . . she had to be careful right now.

"I went to Mexico to investigate misappropriated funds in one of my father's charities, and Rose was the one who helped me discover the truth," Emily said. "I was there for two weeks as I collected the evidence I needed to turn over to the authorities. Rose and I developed an instant friendship."

Torment haunted his gaze. "Rose was like that . . ."

"Did Rose mention any of this?" Emily swallowed hard as she waited to hear what he said.

Mateo nodded. "I was working an assignment three hours away. But she told me what was going on. What a friend of hers had discovered. She talked about someone—Senorita Holcomb. Said you were smart, that you'd discovered corruption that worked its way up the ranks—beyond the organization and into the government even."

"The way the money was hidden was clever. But most of our funding wasn't actually going to the people it was intended for. The people leading this so-called ministry were pocketing it themselves. They were actually connected to the Gemini Cartel."

Mateo's gaze darkened. "When Rose told me

what was going on, I looked into it and had a friend help investigate. That's where I've seen you before. I researched your nonprofit—Graves into Gardens—to make sure it was legit. I saw your picture online. Read articles about you."

They stared at each other, realizing how they were linked.

But it was too much of a coincidence to believe the two of them were together now by chance.

There was more to this. Emily was certain of it.

More memories hit her—memories of the news she'd received after leaving Mexico.

Her throat burned as she said, "I'm so sorry to hear what happened to Rose. I didn't know about it until later. But . . . I was horrified, to say the least. I wasn't expecting that kind of retaliation."

Mateo's jaw flexed. "The cartel members that were still out there wanted to make Rose pay . . ."

Emily started to reach for his arm but stopped herself. She sensed his grief—but she wasn't sure Mateo would accept any comfort. Wasn't sure if she should be the one to offer it either.

Mateo stared at her another moment before stepping back and letting out a long breath. He bent forward as if having trouble accepting this news.

She knew the feeling.

But this was just the beginning.

They had much more to uncover before they discovered the whole truth.

———

Mateo felt an ache pulsing at his temples.

His mind raced through everything he'd just learned.

Then his gaze met Emily's again. "We need to talk this out."

She nodded, looking just as dazed as he felt.

"There's a bench outside." He nodded through the doorway. "Let's go sit there."

Emily followed him to the spot overlooking the pasture. Neither said anything as they walked. No doubt, they were both still processing their connection.

Finally, sitting a comfortable distance away from each other, Mateo started, "Look at these pictures someone sent . . ."

He pulled out his phone and showed her the photos he'd received—photos of Rose and of Emily.

She gasped as she studied the images. "When did you get these?"

"The pictures of Rose? Right before you came. The picture of you? After you were rescued."

Emily glanced up at him, not bothering to hide her confusion. "I don't understand."

Mateo's jaw tightened. "Someone brought you to this area on purpose. They brought you here because they knew I was close. I have a feeling we're both targets in whatever scheme this is."

"But . . ." She shook her head, her entire body tense with apprehension.

"I don't know any details. But if this Arrow guy was part of the Mexican federal police, then maybe he was involved with the corruption surrounding Misión de Comida. I just don't understand why he wants to get even more payback two years later."

"Because of my next investigation . . ." Emily muttered, her shoulders slumping.

His gaze shot up to meet hers. "What investigation?"

"I was scheduled to go to Mexico City to check on one of our ministries there. Before I could go, I was abducted. They threatened me. Said I should back off. I refused. Said I wouldn't back down to bullies."

His eyes widened. "How did they handle that?"

"Not well." She sighed. "I've always thought this corruption was bigger than Misión de Comida. Now, it looks like my impression was correct."

Mateo raked a hand through his hair as his past and his present began to unravel.

CHAPTER 12

Emily watched as Charlie paced her office.

Emily and Mateo had just filled her in about what had happened. Monroe stood in the background, listening and taking in all the details.

"So let me get this straight," Charlie said. "What you're telling me is that someone wanted both of you in the same place to exact revenge. Excuse me for not mincing words, but they already got revenge, didn't they?"

"Something must have changed." Mateo crossed his arms. "And now they want more. Maybe someone in the organization wants to prove themselves or make a statement by coming after us."

"They also want to stop me from pulling donated funds that were actually going toward paying for lavish lifestyles of the people who were supposedly in charge." Emily rubbed her hands against her jeans. "I have a feeling they have their hands in several charities we support in Mexico. It's just one more income stream for them. And the people down there are too afraid to fight them. It's either turn a blind eye or risk death."

Charlie paused and locked gazes with Emily. "How much funding are we talking about?"

"The nonprofit gives millions to ministries, promising to do so with integrity. My father, who started the charity, feels very strongly about that. That's why he hired me to oversee the funding."

"So, these guys who were pocketing this money must have known Mateo was here. They brought you to Arizona because they were planning something—something involving both of you?" Charlie's gaze darkened.

Emily rubbed her lips together as she pondered the question. "I have no idea."

"How did you escape?" Mateo asked as he sat in the chair next to hers.

"A man untied me. Told me I had fifteen minutes to run before people came back. He gave me directions on how to get out of my prison. I didn't have time to ask any questions."

Silence fell for a moment.

"You think he let you go in hopes you'd lead them to Mateo?" Charlie finally asked. "It seems like a stretch, especially since the two of you had never met."

"I agree." Emily bounced her leg nervously. "My gut feeling was that this guy really wanted to help me. And Arrow . . . he wasn't going to let me leave until I agreed to transfer money to another charity that he secretly had his hand in."

"I understand." Charlie started pacing again. "I'm just trying to put the pieces together."

A moment later, Charlie reached into her drawer. "I know I left my map in here . . ."

Emily's skin flushed and she reached into her pocket. "I'm sorry. I took it. I thought it would help me escape, but I still got turned around."

She put the map on the desk.

Charlie glanced at her. "The desert can be deadly —even with a map."

Emily briefly looked at Mateo, wondering what he was thinking. Did he believe her now that she hadn't been in here looking for something else? More importantly, why was she even worried about his opinion of her?

Charlie stretched the map across her desk and pointed to one area at the center of it.

"This is the land I own with Vanishing Ranch."

She outlined and explained that she had two hundred acres she'd already purchased. Then she pointed out an additional two hundred acres, all nestled between the three mountain ranges that surround them. "This is the land that I'm in the process of buying."

Everyone moved closer until they were all leaning over the desk.

"Okay . . ." A knot formed between Mateo's eyes as he stared at the map.

"We don't have any real neighbors out here. But our closest legitimate neighbor is approximately twenty miles away right here." Charlie pointed to a property at the base of the mountain range.

"Who owns that property?" Mateo asked.

"A man named Ron Howell. He's very wealthy. Made money in the alternative energy industry. I try to keep tabs on him, just because it's smart. Apparently, he has several different homes that he splits his time among."

"Picture?" Mateo asked.

She pulled up one on her phone and showed them an image of a man, probably in his fifties, with light-brown hair, a square face, and blue eyes.

Mateo said he didn't recognize him.

"After everything that's happened, I decided to

have Hudson watch his place today," Charlie continued. "No one has been there."

"You think that's where I was being held?" Emily asked.

Charlie shrugged. "It's a good possibility."

"I need to see it, to know if that's true."

As soon as the words left her lips, Mateo adamantly shook his head. "That's a terrible idea. I can take pictures. You don't need to be there."

"But I do. I want to see it. If you're with me, I'll be safe, right?" Emily almost couldn't believe the words had left her lips.

But now that she knew his background—and knew that Rose had loved and trusted him—she felt more comfortable with the man.

Mateo and Charlie exchanged a glance.

And Emily waited for whatever they were going to say.

———

"If you go with Mateo, then you have to play by our rules." Charlie crossed her arms as she turned toward Emily.

Everything in Mateo rebelled against Charlie's words.

Even though he was beginning to trust the

woman more, that didn't mean he wanted her to be a part of any of this. At least, he now knew Emily had been telling the truth when she said she wasn't snooping in Charlie's office.

But still . . .

Emily needed to stay as far away from this as possible. But it was true that they might be able to find answers faster if Emily saw this place with her own eyes.

"I will." Emily nodded affirmatively, her chin set.

Mateo frowned. He'd hoped she would refuse or change her mind.

But the decision was already made. He believed in respecting those in charge, so he didn't argue with Charlie—even though he wanted to.

Instead, he resigned himself to what would happen next. "When do we go?"

Charlie glanced at her watch. "It's already getting dark. Get ready, and we'll leave as soon as possible."

Emily cast him a glance before standing.

Mateo saw the tremble rake through her.

She was nervous about this.

But the woman was also tough, he reminded himself. Much more so than he'd ever guessed.

She'd brought down some powerful people in Mexico. She might be shaken, but she was still a force to be reckoned with. Her abduction had thrown her off-balance. But determination still stretched through her gaze.

She wasn't one to back down to fear . . . or bullies . . . or danger.

He had to admit that he admired those qualities—and they also terrified him.

He only prayed she'd be safe . . .

He felt an unusual protectiveness over the woman. Especially in light of her friendship with Rose.

So that's what he would do.

He would keep her safe.

He just hoped this wasn't a trap.

CHAPTER 13

Twenty minutes later, Mateo and Emily drove toward Ron Howell's place.

He felt a new kinship with Emily. However, he knew this type of bond with her was one neither of them really wanted. It had been born from trauma and loss—ongoing trauma and loss because this wasn't over yet.

"This is a *magnifico* area out here, isn't it?" Mateo kept the conversation generic as he and Emily bounced along the dark desert landscape in his Jeep.

"It's gorgeous." She stared out the window. "If you don't mind me asking, how long have you been working at Vanishing Ranch?"

He shrugged. "Not long. Four months or so."

"You're from Mexico? Your accent isn't strong."

"My mother was American, and my father was

Mexican. We spoke both languages in my house. My parents thought that was very important."

"I'm guessing you have dual citizenship."

"That's correct. My mother's family lives in the Austin area of Texas, so we came up often to visit. But I went to school in Mexico."

Emily stole a glance at him, curiosity in her gaze. "So, were you in Mexico up until four months ago?"

"I've been in the US for the past year. I did some contracting jobs for a while until I came here."

"It's quite the operation you guys have here."

"Charlie is a force to be reckoned with. She's doing a lot of good in the world, and I can't imagine anyone better to head up something like this." Mateo meant the words. As soon as he'd heard about the mission of Vanishing Ranch, he'd been onboard. Charlie hadn't had to work hard to recruit him.

A moment of silence passed as the miles flew by outside.

"By the way, how did the nonprofit get the name Graves into Gardens?" Mateo asked. "From the first time Rose mentioned it to me, I was curious."

"There's actually a song with that name, and we thought it was appropriate for what we were doing," she said. "We're bringing dead things back to life and resurrecting them. We go into areas where there's no hope and bring the hope of Christ by coming alongside ministries already in place and helping them."

"Sounds like a great job."

"It is . . . usually." She glanced at him. "How about you? What's the significance of your tattoo?"

He glanced at his arm. "We lost one of our classmates at the academy in a tragic diving accident. He had this same tattoo, so we all got one in his honor. It helps us to remember the sacrifice he made—and the sacrifice that was required when we took our oath of office."

"I see . . ."

Finally, they pulled up to the house.

Charlie hadn't been exaggerating when she'd told him this man was wealthy.

Mateo thought he'd explored most of the acreage around the ranch. But he'd never seen this place. Maybe it was because the house was partially built into the side of the mountain, and the stoneface siding blended in with the landscape.

He took a mental note that the home was located in the same basic direction where he'd seen those flashlights—and where they'd found that dead body.

The place was also in the same direction Emily had been walking from when he'd found her.

Usually, at a house this size—easily more than ten thousand square feet—hired help was present even when the owner was gone. Sometimes, it was a security guard or a landscaper or housekeeper. But usually there was *someone* around.

This place appeared empty.

They waved to Hudson and exchanged a few words before stashing the Jeep behind some rocks.

Brody, their computer guy, had breached the security system so they could get in unseen. He'd figured out a way to loop the security camera roll so no one would know the feed had been interrupted.

Mateo turned to Emily as they climbed from the Jeep. "Are you ready for this?"

She stared up at him with wide eyes before nodding. "Let's do it."

They carefully approached the side of the house. The shadows were deeper here with the mountain so close, which would help conceal them. They'd already scoped out the door they'd enter.

Brody texted a final confirmation the security system was down.

With that reassurance, Mateo began picking the lock.

They probably had only fifteen minutes to safely get in and out.

"We're in," Mateo muttered, sliding his lock-picking kit back into his pocket and withdrawing his gun instead.

He and Emily stepped inside and paused.

He figured this place would be nice, but it was even grander than he'd imagined.

The floors were all made of polished concrete. The house had an industrial look but with a designer's touch. Mateo didn't know much about art, but the paintings on the wall looked expensive.

The place also didn't appear to be lived in. Nothing was out of place or disturbed. No shoes set beside the door or plates in the sink or keys on the table.

Nor were there any personal pictures.

Did anyone live here?

The whole place felt so . . . cold.

"Anything yet?" he asked.

Emily shook her head. "No, this doesn't look familiar."

The two of them searched room after room, but nothing raised any suspicions. There were no signs that anything nefarious had gone on here. No signs that this was where Emily had been before escaping.

Nothing personal graced this place.

Not in the bedrooms.

Not in the bathrooms.

Not in the office.

Each room left Mateo feeling colder and colder.

Finally, they paused in the kitchen to regroup.

Mateo glanced around. "Something doesn't feel right."

"There's no basement," Emily murmured.

Mateo paused and stared at her. "No basement?"

"A house this size? There's something beneath us. There has to be."

She was right. "Maybe it's hidden."

Emily looked around again. "Where do we even begin looking for a hidden entrance to the basement?"

"I say we look at the most obvious place. How are hidden doorways usually concealed?"

Emily raised her eyebrows. "As cliché as it sounds—in a bookcase."

"Exactly."

They both rushed into the office—where they'd seen bookcases—and began poking around, picking up various objects and pulling different books out from the places on the shelves.

Nothing happened.

Until Mateo pressed against the wooden frame of the unit, and a click sounded.

The entire shelf shifted as if spring-loaded.

———

Emily and Mateo exchanged a glance as they stared at the stairway in front of them. Dim lights had come on when the door opened, barely illuminating the space.

Emily hesitated.

She'd tried to shove aside the memories, to forget what had happened after her abduction. But she no longer had that luxury.

She was going to need to dive in and swim deep if she wanted answers.

And answers meant freedom.

Freedom meant the ability to pursue justice against those who were unjust.

"Does this look familiar?" Mateo asked, glancing down the nondescript stairway.

"Honestly, the place where I was kept was like a dungeon. It was dark. No windows. Cold. The floor felt as if it was stone." She paused and let out a breath, realizing her words hadn't offered much. "They put a hood over my head and didn't take it off until they had me in the room where I stayed. I wish I could tell you more, but . . ."

"You're doing great," Mateo encouraged. "What about when you ran? Did you see anything then?"

"The man pointed me in the right direction. It was a long tunnel—almost like the kind you see in old castles. It was really dark, the air was stale and damp. But the man told me to head left and keep going."

"Keep left? Does that mean there was more than one direction?"

"I wasn't paying a lot of attention. I was too desperate. But I do think there were other directions the passageway went. Anyway, the guy said I'd eventually get out. So that's what I did. I finally reached some type of steel door. When I pushed through it, I was suddenly outside. In the desert. I kept running and never looked back."

Mateo pressed his lips together and nodded as if taking in all of those details. "You don't have to do this."

"I know." An uncontrollable shiver traveled through Emily at the thought of possibly facing the very prison she'd escaped from.

Mateo raised his hand as if to reach for her—to comfort her. But then he pulled away as if thinking better of it.

Instead, Mateo pulled the secret entrance shut behind them, and they walked side by side down the stairs.

Emily braced herself for whatever they would find.

CHAPTER 14

The basement level of the house had been fully converted into living space, Mateo noted.

Not only that, but it had been set up to look like . . . a small town.

The large common area in the center of the space was more of a fake atrium. Lights on the ceiling mimicked sunlight. Benches stood around the edges of an ornate fountain in the middle. Fake trees and other plants had been strategically placed, making the space feel like an outdoor oasis.

The entire place looked like it could be used as a movie set, complete with fake, modern-looking storefronts, houses, and even a post office. Various kinds of siding graced the surfaces as did windows. A wall in the distance had been customized to look like a movie theater. Another to look like an ice cream shop. Another a garage.

"What kind of place is this?" Emily muttered, her arms trembling.

"A doomsayer's lair?" Mateo suggested.

"Maybe. Or it could be the perfect place to hide—or hide someone. It's like an entire faux town—except with no way out."

"It's definitely giving me bad vibes."

Mateo held his gun, afraid of what he might find—or who.

He needed to err on the side of caution.

As he opened the first door, he held his breath.

No one was inside. Instead, it was a room, almost like a hotel with a bed and dresser near the door and a bathroom at the back.

He went room by room and found the same thing.

Each room he saw made him wonder . . .

If people were here by choice, that was one thing.

Against their will? That was an entirely different scenario.

A sick, twisted scenario.

But there were no signs anyone had been in here recently. The covers were smooth. The trash cans empty. The sinks clean.

Had coming here been all for nothing?

That's how it seemed.

There was no evidence that anyone had been kept here—not even Emily.

Which still left the question of where she'd run from.

He had a feeling this bunker wasn't just for safety reasons but because someone liked to keep secrets.

His gut churned as he wondered about what kind of secrets those might be.

He turned to Emily. "Anything ring a bell?"

Emily frowned. "No, I'm sorry."

Just then, a noise caught his ear.

A door slammed.

Upstairs.

Mateo tensed. He instinctively knew the sound hadn't come from Hudson.

No, someone else was here.

———

Panic rushed through Emily.

What if it was Arrow? What if he found her again and tied her up? As she remembered the beatings she'd endured, her head began to spin.

Trembles overtook her as she stood frozen in the middle of the common area with the fountain cheerfully bubbling beside her.

This all seemed so surreal.

But she knew for certain the danger was real.

"Come with me," Mateo muttered.

He took her arm and tugged her into a nearby "house." Once inside, he pressed her against the wall then placed himself in front of her, separating her from the door. He withdrew his gun and raised it, posed to strike if necessary.

Then they listened.

As they did, Mateo grabbed his phone and texted someone. Backup probably.

Emily instinctively clutched Mateo's arm, needing human touch right now to keep her grounded. She pressed her cheek against his back. Air barely filled her lungs.

More footsteps sounded above them.

Someone was walking around the house.

Hudson would have alerted them if someone had approached . . . right?

It didn't make any sense.

Emily heard another door open, this one closer.

The door to the basement, she realized.

Whoever was here was coming closer.

What if he found them?

Panic raced through her at the thought.

CHAPTER 15

ateo glanced at his phone as Hudson texted back his confirmation.

No one has entered or left the house since you arrived.

He squinted. That didn't make any sense. If no one had come or gone, then how was someone here?

Unless there was an entrance they couldn't see.

Mateo's pulse pounded harder.

They would need to figure it out later, but that theory made the most sense.

Right now, Mateo needed to concentrate on keeping Emily safe.

All Mateo had to do was make a phone call, and Hudson would be here to help them. But Mateo hoped the situation wouldn't come down to that. He hoped they could remain hidden and undetected.

Any type of fight may further traumatize Emily. He knew he shouldn't have brought her inside. He shouldn't have brought her here at all—especially since they hadn't even discovered anything.

His heart pounded at a steady but quick rhythm against his ribcage as he waited.

Mateo heard the click of the guy's shoes against the concrete floor as he walked through the common area.

That meant this man wasn't wearing hiking boots or soft-soled shoes.

More likely, he was wearing dress shoes.

Maybe it was the owner of the house, Ron Howell.

Was the man suspicious that someone had broken into his house? Was that why someone was here now? Had a hidden alarm been triggered?

So many questions raced through Mateo's head.

Emily clutched his arm tighter. He could practically feel her fear, and he wished he could comfort her. But he couldn't. Not right now.

Instead, he waited, not daring to make a move. Praying that Emily didn't make any moves in her state of panic.

A shadow crossed the doorway.

The man was mere inches away.

Mateo was tempted to peer around the door and get a glimpse of whoever was here.

But he knew that wouldn't be wise.

Right now, Emily's safety was his main priority.

As the shadow lingered in the doorway, Mateo prepared himself for worst-case scenarios.

———

Emily pressed her eyes closed. She knew the man was close. Knew that one wrong move could mean life or death.

Did that man know they were here?

Mateo had said the home's security system was offline. Nothing should have triggered her and Mateo's arrival.

But the man seemed to be wandering around the basement looking for something.

Or *someone*.

Maybe her.

Her pulse quickened.

Emily could *not* be captured again.

Yet the danger in the air felt palpable.

Mateo remained in front of her, his body still blocking hers as he held his gun.

Time seemed to slow as she waited for what would happen next.

Then she heard a ringing sound.

Panic surged through her.

Was that Mateo's?

A moment later, a deep, rumbling voice came from the other room. "What's going on?"

That sound had been *his* phone. Thank goodness.

Then his voice hit her.

Emily had heard this man somewhere before. When she'd been locked away, she'd been able to hear people talking on the other side of the wall.

He wasn't Arrow, but . . . she felt certain this guy had been one of her captors.

Was this the house where she'd been held captive?

Emily still wasn't sure, but it seemed more and more likely.

CHAPTER 16

"We're losing time here," the man said. "She was never supposed to get away. Find out how she managed that. Someone needs to pay!"

Silence.

"I don't care! I don't want to hear any excuses. I only want answers."

Another pause. Then, "I'm on my way."

Mateo continued to listen.

Finally, the footsteps faded.

The man was leaving.

Mateo's shoulders relaxed slightly. But he couldn't afford to let down his guard.

Instead, he waited.

A door opened.

Footsteps sounded above him.

A few seconds later, another door opened.

Then nothing.

It sounded like the guy was gone, but they still needed to be careful.

Very careful.

He turned slightly to see Emily.

Fear was written all over her features—from her wide eyes to her trembling lips.

He sucked in a breath as her beauty hit him.

Her beauty? That wasn't something he'd expected to notice.

He usually didn't—not since before Rose. No other woman had ever turned his eye.

But Emily, with her wild curls, her sincere eyes, and her fair features, intrigued him entirely more than she should.

He looked away, squeezing her arm instead. He hoped his touch would calm her enough to get through this.

"What now?" Her voice cracked as she whispered the question.

"We need to get out of here before he comes back. Then we can talk about anything else we need to talk about."

She nodded quickly as if anxious to leave.

Still holding his gun with one hand, Mateo took her hand with the other.

He led her through the basement.

They'd exit the way they'd arrived.

Mateo only hoped there were no surprises in the meantime.

He climbed the steps from the basement, opened the door, then looked around.

Everything appeared just as it was when they'd come in earlier.

Maybe that guy truly hadn't known they were here. But, if that was correct, what had he been doing here? Why was he coming and going with so much secrecy?

Clearly, based on what they'd overheard, he was hiding something.

He was definitely connected with Emily.

Moving quickly but carefully, Mateo headed toward the side door. He quietly opened it and pulled Emily out before closing and locking it again.

Then they took off in a run toward the Jeep.

The sooner they were out of here, the better it would be for both of them.

———

Emily's heartbeat slowed as soon as they reached the Jeep.

Hudson—a big guy with kind eyes—waited there for them, gun in hand.

His shoulders loosened when he saw them. "I'm glad you guys are okay. Anything I need to know?"

"I don't know how that guy got in or how he left." Mateo scanned the landscape around them again. "But he was *definitely* in there."

Hudson's gaze darkened. "It looks like we have more work to do."

"My guess is there's another entrance, some kind of tunnel through these mountains, maybe."

"I think you're right," Hudson said. "I've been surprised we haven't seen more vehicles coming and going. Maybe that's why."

"We'll need to explore that possibility. But for now, it's not safe for us to be here." Mateo glanced back at Emily. "I need to get you back to the ranch."

Emily looked as if she wanted to argue.

Then she nodded.

Mateo tucked her inside the Jeep. Then they started down the dark desert road.

Again, he sensed Emily knew something more than she was letting on. He glanced at her. "Is there anything you want to tell me?"

"That man in the house? He's one of them. He was there. In the dungeon. I remember hearing his voice."

CHAPTER 17

When they arrived back at the ranch, Mateo shut off the Jeep's engine and turned to Emily.

He had more questions. But she'd already told him she didn't know who the man was, only that she recognized his voice. She'd just started to relax, and he didn't want to stress her out again.

"I'm going to talk to Charlie and give her the update. Then a few of us are having a bonfire behind the mess hall tonight." He nodded toward the smoke rising in the distance. "I know it seems weird after everything that just happened but . . . there's nothing else we can do tonight, and it's a good way to decompress. Would you like to join us?"

After a moment, she nodded. "I'd love to."

"Great. Why don't you meet me there in about

fifteen? That will give me time to talk to Charlie."

She nodded, and Mateo walked her to her guesthouse before heading back to the mess hall.

He gave Charlie the update before grabbing two hot chocolates and heading to the fire.

Just as he arrived and got settled, Emily appeared, a flannel blanket wrapped over her shoulders.

She lowered herself onto the bench beside him, a comfortable two feet away. He handed her the cup of cocoa, and she murmured thank you before staring into the dancing flames in front of her.

She seemed lost in thought. She had many good reasons to be.

Mateo did some of his best thinking while staring at the flames.

Maybe she did also.

Monroe was here with his guitar, and he played a few songs. Several people joined him and sang, while others remained quiet.

As he started to strum "The Old Rugged Cross," Emily began to sing along.

Her voice was so crystal clear that everyone else stopped singing and listened to her.

She knew every verse.

The look on her face showed she meant every word she sang.

Warmth filled Mateo's chest.

There was something special about this woman. There was no doubt about that. Even Rose had thought so. She'd spoken highly of Emily.

He'd had his doubts at first, but the more he learned, the more impressed he was by her *integridad*.

When the song ended, a round of applause for Emily erupted. She blushed but smiled at the reaction.

Several minutes later, Monroe packed up his guitar, and everyone else faded away, heading back to their accommodations for the night.

But Mateo and Emily remained.

He shifted his gaze to the fire as they both watched the flames crackle and dance. The warmth helped to ward off the slight chill in the air. A brief moment of peace washed over him as he temporarily set his troubles aside.

"There's more to my story," Emily finally said, her voice quiet and reflective.

"I figured there might be."

She remained quiet several minutes.

"You don't have to share," Mateo said.

Emily sucked in a deep breath before slowly nodding. "Maybe I don't *have* to. But I need to."

———

Emily couldn't believe she was sharing her story.

She hadn't told anyone these details. But she knew she couldn't stay quiet any longer.

She wished it hadn't taken her this long to speak up about the trauma she'd gone through. Wished she was the open-book type who easily shared her story in order to help others.

But being the daughter of a well-known pastor . . . she'd come to appreciate her privacy, especially in a world where so many were easily offended or looking for someone to judge. Discretion had almost become a survival tactic.

"My father pastors a large church in Los Angeles," she started. "I'm sure you've probably heard of the congregation. Grand Haven Community."

"Sounds familiar." He poked the fire.

"Please, don't judge me for what I'm about to tell you." Her voice cracked with emotion as she gazed at the fire and tried to gather her courage.

"I'm not perfect, Emily. I don't have the right to judge anyone." Mateo sounded sincere, like he was humble enough to try to understand the places different people were at in their lives.

She hoped that was true.

She drew in another shaky breath before speaking again.

"A couple of months ago, I met this guy named

Kyle." Her voice trembled as she said his name. "Even though I'm twenty-seven, I haven't dated much. People always give me a hard time and say my standards are too high. But the truth is that I'm not willing to settle. I don't think I should have to. But something about Kyle was different."

Mateo's brown eyes were kind and compassionate as he listened.

Just yesterday, Emily couldn't imagine telling this story to anyone—definitely not Mateo, of all people.

But today, she knew she couldn't keep this secret any longer.

"I met Kyle at a church event, and he seemed like the perfect Christian guy. He knew all the right language, he knew the Bible, and he treated me like gold." She sucked in a breath before continuing. "There were some warning signs, I suppose. Like the fact I never met any of his friends or family. But he said he'd just moved to the area, so it made sense to me at the time. Anyway, he asked me out the day we met. We went out that next Friday. The following week we saw each other three times. It was like we had this instant connection, one that I'd never experienced before."

She stared into the fire, again trying to find the courage to finish.

Her hands began shaking as she started the next

part of her story. "A few weeks ago, Kyle took me to dinner at a fancy restaurant. The way he was acting, I knew he'd planned something big. I even briefly wondered if he was thinking about proposing, which would've been crazy since we hadn't known each other that long. But there was just something in the air that I couldn't put my finger on."

She paused and drew in a shaky breath.

Finally, she continued. "Halfway through my entrée, I realized I wasn't feeling like myself. I don't even remember leaving the restaurant. But when I woke up, I was in my apartment."

"Was Kyle there?"

Emily's insides began quaking, and nausea rose inside her. She thought for sure she might throw up right there, but she didn't.

She still could. It wasn't too late.

"No. He was gone, and I was . . . I was . . . naked." Her voice trailed as humiliation returned in full force, as it did every time she thought of what happened.

Mateo's eyes widened.

A tear rolled down Emily's cheek, and she wasn't sure if she was going to be able to continue.

There were a lot of ways people could be traumatized.

What had been done to her felt like one of the worst.

CHAPTER 18

"It's okay," Mateo said. "You don't have to tell me more."

He saw the stress on Emily's face and didn't want to make her relive this trauma.

If he knew her better or if their circumstances were different, he might reach over and squeeze her hand or even give her a hug.

But he knew that wouldn't be appropriate.

Instead, he did the only thing he could.

He listened.

"The thing is, I'm not one of those girls who sleeps around." Emily used the back of her hand to wipe beneath her eyes. "I'm the kind who's saving myself for marriage. I know it sounds old-fashioned, but—"

"I think it's very admirable," Mateo said.

Her shoulders relaxed as she stared at him, appearing to find comfort in his words.

"So, Kyle and I hadn't slept together. That's why I didn't understand where my clothes were, or where Kyle was, or how I ended up back at home. Nothing made sense. That's not to mention the fact I had a killer headache."

"He drugged you." Mateo stated his conclusion as a fact.

Emily nodded. "He must've put something in my drink. I never even considered he might do something like that. In fact, when I woke up, I was initially concerned about him. I thought something had happened, that he might be hurt. I later realized that wasn't the case."

Mateo felt his fists tightening with every new detail. Guys like Kyle made Mateo sick to his stomach.

"I didn't think anything . . . anything . . . *physical* had happened between Kyle and me. I didn't understand why he would drug me and . . ." She paused and cleared her throat. "Then my phone buzzed on the nightstand. I got a text message. There were . . . there were pictures there. A lot of pictures." Another tear rolled down her cheek, and she wrapped her arms around her middle, seeming to shrink before his eyes.

Mateo had a feeling he knew exactly what kind of pictures they were, but he waited for Emily to continue.

"They were very . . . provocative. They were only of me. I would've never . . ." She buried her face in her hands as her tears turned into sobs.

His heart thudded against his chest. "You don't have to do this . . ."

It went against his nature to sit still. To not move toward her and pull her into his arms.

"I haven't told anyone what happened. No one. I've just been living in shame for the past three weeks."

"What Kyle did to you was horrible," Mateo said. "I've only known you a few days, but I feel confident that anyone who knows you well knows you wouldn't have had those pictures taken of your own accord."

"My eyes were closed in almost all of them. But . . . the pictures were horrifying. The text said that the photos would be sent to my friends and family unless I did exactly what I was told. I asked what he wanted from me. He said *they'd* be in touch." Emily drew in another shaky breath. "That's when I knew there were others involved. It wasn't just Kyle doing this. I felt so ashamed."

Guys like these preyed on people's shame. They

knew how to manipulate. That's why they were so good at what they did.

When Rose had first gone to work for the charity, she'd thought the leadership was upstanding also. Then she'd begun to realize that their words and actions didn't seem to measure up. She'd noticed the nice clothes, the new cars, the bigger homes.

When Emily had come to check on the organization, Rose had told Emily her observations. Emily was the one who had access to the mission's financials. Together, the two women had discovered the truth.

Emily had been the one to go to the authorities.

His throat tightened with emotion—and anger—at the thought of the end results.

Mateo cleared his throat. He wanted to go find these guys. To teach them a lesson. To make sure they could never hurt Emily—or anyone else—again.

Instead, for now, he asked, "What did they want you to do?"

Emily dragged her gaze up to meet his, and Mateo knew that whatever it was, it was even more painful than seeing those pictures.

———

Emily wasn't sure if it felt good to get the truth off her chest or if she was just reliving a nightmare. In reality, it was a little of both.

But she'd come this far, and she couldn't stop now.

However, she could no longer look Mateo in the eye after what she'd told him. Instead, she stared into the flames.

"The message said that I needed to turn a blind eye to some indiscretions I was looking into as part of my job. That if I didn't, I would pay the price—in a worse way than those photos."

His eyes narrowed. "What happened next?"

Emily sucked in a deep breath, something comforting about the smoky scent in the air. "I didn't say anything at first. I hoped it was just a bad joke. I didn't know. I was in panic mode—torn between my integrity and my reputation. I was between the proverbial rock and hard place."

Out of the corner of her eye, she saw Mateo glance at her. "You must have feared the backlash of either choice."

"And the humiliation." Emily continued staring at the dancing flames in front of her. "Those pictures would embarrass my family. Hurt my father's ministry. And I wouldn't want to ever show my face again around any of my friends or the people at church. Even if they heard the truth and believed it, those images would still be in their mind, and I couldn't handle that."

"What did you do then?"

"A few weeks passed, and nothing happened. I thought maybe it was just a bad joke." She swallowed hard. "Then they texted again, asking about my choice. I told them I couldn't turn a blind eye to corruption. When I got into my car that day after work, someone was in the back seat. He sprayed something in my face, and everything went black."

"Take your time," Mateo muttered. "You don't have to tell me anything you're not comfortable with."

She appreciated that, but she'd already started and couldn't stop now. "When I woke up my hands and feet were tied to a chair, and I was in some kind of basement with a man who'd introduced himself as Arrow and some other men I'd never seen before."

"Did they . . . ?" Mateo's voice trailed off as if he couldn't finish the question.

Nausea pooled in Emily's stomach. His question was expected, an assumption anyone would make. But . . . it still made her feel sick to her stomach.

She stared at her hands as they rested in her lap. "Arrow talked about things his guys were going to do to me. But he said they had other purposes for me first. I escaped before any of that happened."

Mateo's expression remained stony. "Did he say what those other purposes were?"

"No. He said he would reveal his plan to me soon enough."

His hands fisted and unfisted as if her story deeply disturbed him. As if he wanted to jump in and teach those guys a lesson. As if he understood just how dire the situation had been.

"What happened next?" His voice sounded strained as he asked the question.

"Then I got away, and you found me. Now, here we are."

CHAPTER 19

Mateo rocked back on the bench, his mind racing.

He could see why Emily had been hesitant to share her story. These guys were doing what they did best. They'd humiliated her. Took away her pride. Left her completely exposed and at their mercy.

But who had cut her free? Had one of the traffickers had a change of heart? Was someone there working undercover? Or had someone let her go on purpose so Mateo could find her? Obviously, these guys were going to connect them at some point.

Mateo didn't know, and he supposed that answer wasn't really important right now. What was important was that Emily was safe.

And he needed to keep her that way.

Emily finally glanced at him. "I'm starting to feel like I can trust you. I mean, I thought I could trust Kyle—"

"I'm nothing like Kyle."

She stared at him a moment before frowning. "The problem is, Kyle would've said that same thing. He always acted so chivalrous, like he hated it when men treated women poorly. I bought every lie he sold me."

"I understand that trust has to be earned. But I'm grateful you trusted me enough to share this."

"It helps that I knew your wife. She . . . thought the world of you." Her gaze pitched up to meet his, and she sighed. "Now that you know, what are you going to do with this information?"

Mateo tried to choose his words carefully. "What do you want me to do? It's not my call to make."

Emily rubbed her hands together, her anxiety obvious—and understandable. "The thing is . . . I'm not thinking straight right now. I just don't know what's gotten into me. But suddenly, my decision-making ability is gone."

"That's normal considering the trauma you've been through. I can help you navigate through this. If that's what you want."

She shrugged as if resigned. "That would be . . . helpful. I feel . . . lost."

"Let me ask you this." Mateo shifted on the bench. "The team here has searched online, and we haven't seen anything about your disappearance. I've got to assume you're close to your family. Why haven't they reported you missing?"

"They expected me to be out of the country. I was supposed to leave the next morning for Mexico City. I usually travel alone—except for a bodyguard—and I was supposed to be gone for a week. I'm sure they didn't think anything about it. I usually don't call them when I'm away—not unless something important comes up."

Mateo turned toward her, knowing he needed to seize this opportunity. "Emily, if you tell your parents what happened, that will take away the power these pictures have over you."

"I don't know . . ."

"It's okay if you decide not to." Mateo lowered his voice, knowing he couldn't push too hard. "But if you decide to call them, I'll be right there by your side, if you want."

"Thanks . . ." She stuttered some as she said the word.

"Is it okay with you if I share this with Charlie?"

Emily let out a long breath. "It's probably best that she knows. I'd like to be there when you tell her. In case she has any . . . questions."

"Why don't you sleep on it, and then we can talk to her in the morning?"

"That sounds good. Thank you." She offered a fleeting smile. "You know, Rose always said you were a great listener. She said it was one of the first things that made her fall in love with you—along with your dashing good looks, of course."

A sad smile tugged at his lips. "The truth is that Rose was always out of my league."

Something flashed in Emily's eyes, but she looked away, seeming to mentally shift gears. "I know you need to put out the fire. I'll walk myself to my guesthouse."

Mateo stood when she did. He was still tempted to pull her into his arms. To comfort her. But he wasn't sure that's the kind of comfort she needed right now. He'd meant it when he'd said he'd help her navigate through this. He just wasn't sure exactly what that would look like.

Instead, he simply said good night.

When she was gone, Mateo let out a breath. His thoughts raced as he reviewed what he'd learned and the ordeal Emily had been through.

First, the pictures.

Then she'd been abducted. Held captive.

But thankfully, she'd escaped.

Rose had also been abducted. Held captive. But

she'd been killed.

A headache began to pulse in his head.

Nausea welled in him as he remembered his late wife and what she'd gone through when ruthless, evil men had shown her no mercy.

His hands fisted again.

He hadn't been able to save his wife. But he vowed that wouldn't be the case with Emily.

For some reason, it comforted him to know that Rose and Emily had known each other. He was glad they'd been able to support each other during the investigation into Misión de Comida.

Just as he poured a bucket of water on the bonfire, a scream cut through the air.

It wasn't Emily.

No, it sounded like a little girl.

———

Emily heard the scream and ran toward the door of her guesthouse.

She burst outside in time to see Mateo running across the common area.

"Stay in your room!" he yelled over his shoulder.

Emily knew she should. But she couldn't seem to stop herself from gravitating toward the sound.

As she rounded the corner, she spotted a little girl

and her mom standing outside one of the guest-houses. The little girl was crying hysterically.

Emily froze and listened.

"There was a giant lizard out there." The girl's voice cracked with frenzied emotion as she pointed beyond the gate.

Mateo knelt in front of her, the picture of patience and concern.

The sight of it made Emily's heart skip a beat.

Others had also wandered out and formed a loose circle around them.

"Honey." The girl's mom gripped her arms. "There are lizards in the desert. It's okay."

The girl's chin trembled. "No, you don't understand. It was big."

Her mom let out a weak, almost embarrassed laugh. She clearly didn't like the attention this was bringing them. "There are big lizards out here too. They won't hurt you. Now, let's get back inside and let these people get their rest—"

"No! You don't understand. It was big. As big as a person."

Emily froze at the sound of that.

As big as a person? Had the girl been having a nightmare?

Mateo seemed to follow that same train of thought.

He glanced up at the mother. "Did she drift to sleep?"

"No, we were reading a book. Anna got up to go to the bathroom and glanced out the window. She likes to see if she can view the Milky Way sometimes. That's when she screamed."

Mateo glanced back at two of his teammates—Jesse and Hayes, if Emily remembered correctly. The two men started toward the gate, no doubt to see if there was anything out there to be worried about.

Emily would definitely say that lizard people seemed to be something that might be a concern.

The problem was lizard people didn't exist.

Not unless you were in an episode of *Scooby-Doo*.

A chill washed over her.

Was there anywhere that was truly safe?

Emily felt certain the answer to that was no.

CHAPTER 20

Charlie escorted the girl and her mother back into their guesthouse, but not before whispering for Mateo to also check out whatever had happened outside the fence.

Several guys would patrol the area near the guesthouses.

But he, Jesse, and Hayes were going to see if trouble was really close or if the little girl was having an episode. Meanwhile, Monroe would check the security-camera footage. If anyone had gotten close to the ranch, an alarm should have alerted them.

Mateo wanted to know why the alarm hadn't sounded. If, in fact, there had been someone out there. Then again, whoever had left Rose's engagement ring on the fence had slipped past also.

His gut clenched at the thought of it.

With one more glance back at Emily to make sure she was okay, Mateo joined Jesse and Hayes near the fence.

Jesse Marx was former FBI, and Hayes Barlow former Homeland Security. Hayes was the newer team member who'd been brought in as the needs and demands of Vanishing Ranch had grown. Charlie was hiring more people.

Jesse pointed at something on the ground with the beam of his flashlight.

"It looks like the soil has been disturbed," Jesse said. "It's hard to tell for sure out here because it's so dry, but the dust has been kicked up and this plant has been trampled."

"By a lizard man?" Mateo stared at his two colleagues and waited for their reaction.

Jesse shrugged. "Stranger things have happened. I'm up for checking it out. Seems a little bit lighter than most of the stuff we deal with. And there *are* those out there who think lizard people exist. I remember hearing the story of that guy from California who killed his kids because he thought they had serpent DNA in them. I don't know what's going on in people's heads sometimes."

Mateo rubbed his jaw, perplexed—and disgusted—at how messed up some people could be. "If someone was out here, then where did he go? If this person ran away, it seems like someone would've seen something."

The three of them turned and surveyed the area around them.

It was nearly pitch-black out here, and the darkness could conceal a lot. But it did seem like a stretch that someone had been here and able to escape so quickly. If this person had come in a car or on a UTV, they would've heard it.

That's when another mark on the ground caught Mateo's eye.

He knelt beside it for a better look. "Do you see this? It's barely discernible, but I think it's there."

Jesse squatted beside him. "This is from a bicycle tire, isn't it?"

Mateo's jaw tightened again. "Somebody *was* here. That's how he got away—via bicycle."

"I'll get the Jeep out and see if I can find him." Hayes took a step toward the gate.

Jesse rose and walked toward the gate also. "I'll go with you."

"And I'll check in with Monroe to see if he picked up on anything on the security cameras." Mateo paused. "One way or another, we'll get to the bottom of this."

"You've got to be kidding me." Mateo shook his head as he stared at the computer screen in Charlie's office.

Sure enough, what appeared to be a human-size lizard rode a bike toward the ranch. The creature got off and peered in the gate. Anna's scream cut through the air, sending the lizard man pedaling away.

Mateo had never seen anything like it except maybe in a movie.

"How did this thing get past the alarms?" Mateo muttered.

"We need someone to go out there tomorrow to double-check our sensors." Monroe rubbed his jaw as he stared at the screen. "I can definitively say that we've never had this problem before."

"I've seen a lot of crazy things," Mateo said. "Some of the things that happened when I worked in Mexico . . . you would shake your head if you knew, especially during the Festival of the Dead. And I haven't even mentioned the chupacabra yet."

"People like to tell unusual stories out here in the desert," Monroe said. "They're superstitious people. There's talk of skin-walkers that date back to the Navajos. This area wasn't tribal land, but the legend has still extended here."

"Did you guys figure out anything?" Charlie

strode into the office with a cup of steaming coffee in her hands.

Mateo wasn't sure how the woman was always so alert. She was always ready and willing to talk, no matter the time of day or night.

The guys around here—affectionately referred to as Charlie's Angels—often said that was her superpower.

Monroe showed Charlie the video, and she shook her head as she stared at the screen. A knot formed between her eyes, and a new heaviness fell over her.

"Whatever is going on here, I don't like it," she murmured. "We are going to have to up our efforts. We're not going to be taken down by some . . . by some . . ." She twirled her finger in the air as if trying to find the right words. "Some *wannabe reptile person.*"

Mateo rolled his shoulders back. "Whatever you need from us, you just let us know."

"I will." Still holding her coffee, Charlie loosely crossed her arms as she stared at the screen. "Right now, we need to get to the bottom of whatever is going on with Emily. Someone could be out there looking for her . . . and maybe they'd even resort to dressing like a lizard to do so."

CHAPTER 21

Emily woke up more determined than ever to discover exactly what was going on.

Before going to bed, she'd spent much of the night on her knees—literally—praying for wisdom about the situation. *Be as shrewd as a snake but as innocent as a dove.* That had been her mantra with her job. That needed to be her mantra now also.

As she opened her eyes this morning, she knew what she had to do.

She quickly got dressed and went to the mess hall. As she approached Charlie's office, she was surprised to see Monroe there.

He glanced up at her and flashed something that bore a small resemblance to a smile. "Can I help you?"

"I'd like to use a computer. And maybe even get a cell phone."

He nodded slowly as he seemed to process her words. "Okay."

"Is that against the rules?"

"No, it's not against the rules. But it's gonna take me a few minutes to get a computer and cell phone set up for you. We have to take precautions so they can't be traced. Why don't you grab breakfast first?"

That sounded like a decent plan, despite her impatience.

Thankfully, as she stepped into the cafeteria, she spotted Mateo.

Her heart raced at the sight of him.

Raced? No, she couldn't let her heart go there.

Yet it already had.

In the short time that she had known the man, he was already earning a place in her heart. The realization was crazy and unexpected. Emily was sure it wouldn't lead to anything.

But she knew he was a good man.

She knew that not only from her short time with him here at the ranch, but from everything that Rose had ever said about him.

The two had been married eight years, and the woman had still had only glowing things to say about her husband.

That was admirable, especially since it seemed so many were eager to rip their spouses to shreds—although often hidden beneath humor or sarcastic remarks. A marriage where a man and woman respected each other was a blessing—and a goal.

Mateo paused in front of her, a haunted look in his eyes. "Hey. How did you sleep?"

"Not great. Too much on my mind."

"Me too." He rubbed his chin. "Why don't you grab a plate, and we can go into the spare office? I want to show you something."

Her heart pounded harder. Did he have an update for her?

Emily hoped so.

She grabbed a bagel, some cream cheese, and some fruit. Then she filled up an extra-large cup with coffee and followed Mateo into an empty office next to Charlie's.

Mateo had a computer already set up on the table, and he motioned for her to sit beside him.

She did, carefully setting her food and drink on the other side of the laptop. As she peered at the screen, her arm brushed Mateo's, and a shot of electricity went through her.

She quickly drew her arm back wondering if he'd felt the same thing.

Instead, she cleared her throat as she turned to him. "What's going on?"

"I found pictures of the guys that I went to the academy with. If you don't mind, I'd like you to look through them and tell me if any seem familiar."

Her breath caught.

Was she ready to see Arrow's face again?

The thought of it caused a cold shudder to grip her.

She had to face the possibility that one of these guys might be him. It would be a good thing if she recognized him. She needed to identify his real name so they could track him down.

"Okay, I'm ready." As ready as she could be, anyway.

Emily picked up her cup of coffee and lifted a quick prayer.

———

An hour later, Mateo and Emily hadn't made any progress. He'd shown her each of the twelve people who'd gotten the same tattoo.

None of them were familiar to her.

None of them were Arrow.

Mateo had to admit he was disappointed.

"What can you tell me about this Arrow guy?"

Mateo took mental notes of everything, knowing each detail could help him track down these people. "How did he look?"

"He was on the taller side and muscled—but not so many muscles that he appeared intimidating. It was the look in his eyes that was threatening. The man seemed . . . soulless, I suppose. His black eyes were like an abyss." She let out another breath, one that almost sounded like a chuckle. "I know it sounds dramatic, but it's true. Anyone who saw him on the street probably wouldn't notice. He otherwise looked respectable."

Mateo had met plenty of guys like Arrow in his line of work. They were the devil in sheep's clothing. He despised how they preyed on anyone they perceived as weaker.

But he didn't remember anyone who fit that description who'd worked with Misión de Comida. However, the leadership was tied in with the Gemini Cartel. Mateo had shot and killed their leader, Miguel Sanchez, when the man had fired at officers while resisting arrest. Many others were now behind bars.

That didn't mean that others from the cartel weren't out there.

He swallowed hard. "Anything else you can remember? An accent or scar or a tattoo besides the one you told me about?"

"He did have a scar on his temple." Emily ran her hand across the skin near her hairline on the left side of her face. "Right here. I know that probably doesn't help much . . ."

"Every little bit helps." Mateo leaned back and frowned as he thought everything through.

Who else would have had that same tattoo besides the people he'd gone to the academy with? It didn't make sense.

But Emily sounded confident that none of the men were familiar.

That pretty much left them back at square one.

As Mateo glanced at her, he saw the disappointment on her face as well.

He ran a hand over his eyes.

He'd been up for most of the night checking the trigger alarms near the fence line.

One of the sensors had been smashed with a rock. That's how the lizard man had gotten past it.

Jesse was heading out this morning to check on the other sensors around the ranch and make sure they were all working properly.

Mateo didn't like the fact that danger was inching closer to this area—this sanctuary. He closed his computer and turned toward Emily. "Listen, how about we take a quick horseback ride? It might help us clear our thoughts."

She frowned. "A horseback ride seems like a luxury when time is of the essence right now."

"It's amazing sometimes what will come to you when you just take a step back for a moment. It won't be a long ride. Maybe an hour. But I think it'll be good for both of us. Do you ride?"

"Not really."

"I'll teach you. It's not hard."

She still hesitated but finally nodded.

Twenty minutes later, they were saddled up and riding in the pasture. Emily had caught on easily, just as he'd guessed she would. The day was perfect—not too hot or cold. The sun cast an orange light around them, magnifying the beautiful colors of the desert.

He glanced at Emily. She was a sight to see on horseback and looked like a real natural. Rose had once liked horseback riding, but she'd been thrown from a mare in her early twenties and had never wanted to ride after that.

They'd had a lot of happy memories riding together, and he hadn't realized until now how much he missed that.

"I have been thinking this through all night," Mateo said as he gripped The Lone Ranger's reins. "When you go to these places overseas to investigate, do you go alone?"

Emily shook her head. "No, my father didn't

think that would be safe, especially considering some of the places that I was visiting. I usually took a bodyguard with me."

His eyebrows flickered up. "A bodyguard? The same person each time?"

"Yes. His name was Tucker Munslow. But he quit . . . two weeks ago." Her face went pale as she said the words. "Do you think . . . ?"

His shoulder twitched up. "I think it's a good possibility, one that's worth exploring."

"I agree. I can't believe I never put that together. But Tucker said he got another job offer, and I just assumed . . ."

"It just seems if these guys are determined enough to go to such extremes to get what they want, that they might try to buy this guy too. Someone clearly knew who you are and where you live and a lot about you." He paused. "You said you were supposed to go on another trip. Who were you taking with you if Tucker quit?"

"I was looking for someone else to hire, but I hadn't finalized anything. My dad asked me about it, and I told him I had it handled. I found this private security organization called Blackout, and I was going to hire them. Honestly, I thought I might have to delay my trip, but I didn't tell anyone that."

Emily stole a quick glance at him. "Are they

trying to get revenge on both of us? Is that why they brought me here of all places?"

Mateo's gut tightened. "That's what I've been wondering about as well. I think it's a good possibility. You were the one who made these guys lose millions—in their eyes. And I killed their leader. To me, it seems as if they're trying to not only control you and the funds that this ministry is scheduled to give to these people, but they also want to send a message."

Emily frowned. "I just don't like any of this."

"I don't either, but we're going to get to the bottom of this. When we get back, I'll look into your bodyguard. I need to know where he is right now."

She nodded, even though the motion seemed weak. "Okay. And if it's all right . . . I would like to check on my parents. I've been praying about it, and I think it's the right thing to do. I don't think these guys have involved them, but I need to make sure."

"I think that's a good decision."

CHAPTER 22

ack at the ranch, Monroe gave Emily the laptop and cell phone she'd requested.

She and Mateo went back to the spare office and sat down.

Before making any phone calls, Emily pulled up the internet browser and did a quick search for her family's name to see if there was any news. If there was anything she'd missed. If perhaps her disappearance had been reported or those photos had been leaked.

She found nothing.

Even though Emily should have felt better, she didn't.

She'd halfway expected something. But after she'd escaped, it appeared that these guys had gone silent.

Were they looking for her?

They didn't seem like the type to just simply let her run and do nothing about it. Especially when they knew she had information that could bring them down.

Next, she picked up her cell phone, a burner that wouldn't be able to be traced back to her or the ranch.

She stared at the screen a moment, her mouth dry at the thought of talking to her parents and telling them what was happening.

"Second thoughts?" Mateo studied her.

She rubbed a hand over her face. "If my parents don't know any of this . . . I want to protect them. I don't want them to know what I've been through."

"I'm sure they care about what happens to you."

"I know they care about me." Emily paused and nibbled on her bottom lip a moment. "But we lost my older sister a few years ago to breast cancer, and I saw how much they struggled. If I can save them from any of that pain then that's all I want to do. I know that it might not make any sense—"

Mateo's hand covered hers. "It makes all the sense in the world. You do whatever you think you need to do."

Her heart pounded faster at Mateo's touch.

He seemed to realize what he'd done and withdrew his hand. Emily immediately missed his warmth, missed the connection.

She hadn't realized how alone she'd felt since her older sister died. How much she'd just been working so she wouldn't have to think about her loss. But what had happened over the past couple of days had forced her to examine herself and her life.

She'd been working too much. Trying too hard to bury her pain. But now it was bubbling to the surface.

She pushed back tears and averted her gaze back to her phone.

She wouldn't call her parents, she decided. Instead, she'd call a friend who worked at the church with her father and who knew her whole family.

If there was anything she needed to know, Abigail would tell her.

Emily dialed the number and, a moment later, her friend answered.

"Aren't you supposed to be in Mexico?" Abby asked, her cheerful voice sounding on the line.

"Yes, but I just had this urge to check on everything back at home. I can't explain it. You know how you just get those feelings sometimes?" Emily's words were mostly the truth, though she felt guilty for her omissions.

"I get that. But everything seems to be fine here."

A moment of relief filled Emily. If Abigail had seen those photos, she would sound different right now . . . right? But nothing in her voice indicated that she knew anything was going on with Emily.

Emily shifted in her chair. "That's good to hear. What about my parents? Have you seen them lately?"

"Funny that you ask that. Your dad actually called in sick for work the past couple of days."

Alarm raced through her. "Is everything okay?"

"Maybe he just needed some time off."

"I'm sure that's probably what it is," Emily quickly corrected before her friend got suspicious. "I'm just surprised he didn't mention it before I left."

"Well, I'm sure it's nothing. Sometimes bad gut feelings turn out not to be anything except paranoia. Am I right?"

She knew her friend was trying to make her feel better.

But in this case, the bad feeling in Emily's gut was absolutely correct.

She ended the call and turned to Mateo. "I need to go visit my parents."

A knot formed between his eyes. "You don't want to call them?"

"No, I need to see them with my own eyes . . . and I want to talk to Tucker."

Mateo stared at her another moment before nodding. "Okay. I'll see what I can do."

———

An hour later, Mateo and Emily were in his Jeep and on the road.

Mateo prayed this went well, especially since he had reservations about this trip. But Emily had insisted, and he wanted to respect her choices.

He glanced over at her now as she rode beside him. She'd donned some jeans and a lightweight black sweater along with cowboy boots.

The look was . . . nice.

Then again, Mateo liked the way she looked in a T-shirt and shorts also.

He hadn't expected to feel attracted to this woman. But he did.

Knowing that Rose had known her only made his bond with Emily feel stronger.

He knew that the reason she wore long sleeves was probably to cover her injuries. She'd also put on some makeup, carefully concealing the bruises on her face. He knew she did so to protect her family from the reality of what she'd been through.

Her love and concern for them was touching.

Mateo averted his thoughts and asked, "How are your wrists healing?"

Emily glanced at him and then at her wrists. "They're getting better. They don't hurt anymore. My face is starting to look halfway normal as well." She smoothed down her hair and fidgeted with her clothes.

"I can tell you're nervous. That's normal."

"I know." She rubbed her arms. "I don't know if I'm more nervous about seeing my parents or about the possibility of my worst fears being true and finding out something happened to them."

He gripped the steering wheel as they bounced over the desert landscape. "If something happened to them or they disappeared, we would've most likely heard. You can't pastor a church of that size and just disappear without making headlines."

"That's true. I suppose that makes me feel a little better."

He stole another glance at her. "Do you mind if I ask you a couple more questions?"

"Go ahead. But I can't promise I'll answer."

Mateo noted how she rubbed her arms again, drawing them into herself.

"Fair enough." He was going to need to tread carefully. Her emotions could make her fragile.

"While you were being held captive . . . did you see Kyle?"

A frown tugged at her lips. "No, I didn't. It was like he disappeared into thin air."

"You said something about learning that Kyle worked for Arrow. How did you know that?"

"Arrow told me. He rubbed it in my face that I'd been naive."

"Did you get the impression Arrow was the head honcho in the operation?"

"No, not at all. In fact, he took a couple of phone calls from someone else. I think there's a whole pyramid of people, and Arrow was above Kyle, but there was also someone—at least one person—above Arrow. But maybe more than that."

Of course. These guys had networks they tapped into.

They continued to head west from the ranch, driving toward LA. They had about a four-hour ride ahead of them. The roads were mostly barren, the landscape morphing from flat desert to hilly with gorges, mesas, and canyons.

His foot hit the brakes when he saw a truck pulled to the side of the road near a gas station up ahead. Two men stood beside it, flagging drivers down as they passed.

Alarm raced through him.

"Mateo?" Emily's voice cracked as she stared out the window.

"Listen, I'm going to need for you to get in the back seat."

"What?" Surprise laced her voice.

"I don't have time to explain. But lie on the floor of the back seat and cover yourself with a blanket. Hurry."

She glanced at him another second before springing into action.

And she was just in time.

One of the men stepped into the road right in front of them, forcing Mateo to either stop or hit him.

Mateo lowered one hand, reaching for the gun he kept in his door.

He didn't want to use it . . . but he would if he had to.

CHAPTER 23

Emily felt her heart pounding in her ears.

What was going on? Who were those men, and why were they stopping people in the middle of this road?

Whatever the reason, Mateo was clearly concerned.

That meant she was concerned also.

She felt the Jeep slowing. A moment later, it came to a complete stop.

Then she heard the wind rushing in as Mateo rolled down his window. "Can I help you?"

"Sorry to stop you," a deep voice said. "But we're looking for this woman. We believe she may have been abducted."

Paper rattled, and silence stretched a moment.

"I'm sorry to hear she's missing," Mateo

murmured. "This area is usually so safe, from what I understand. Hopefully, the county sheriff is helping you look for her. But I don't recognize her."

"The sheriff is helping. But we can't just sit around and wait for them to find her. We have to do something, you know?"

Emily held her breath.

Were they showing Mateo a picture of her?

Probably.

She'd heard that voice somewhere before, but she couldn't place it.

She was careful not to move, not to draw any attention just in case these guys looked in the back seat.

"Is she from around here?" Mateo asked.

"Yes, she lives about twenty minutes from here," the man said.

"Can I keep this flyer?" Mateo asked. "Just in case I see her. I can give you a call."

"Yeah, man. That sounds great."

As another moment of silence stretched, Emily held her breath.

What was the guy doing? Had he seen her? Was he looking in the back seat?

She pressed her eyes closed and began to pray.

———

Mateo remained tense but tried not to show it as the second guy walked around the Jeep, clearly peering in the back seat.

Could he see Emily back there?

If so, things might turn ugly fast.

Mateo's hand remained at his side, his gun just within reach in case he needed to use it.

"You from around here?" the man who'd handed him the flyer finally asked.

Mateo tried to relax his shoulders and voice. "Just moved to the area a few months ago."

It was best to try to stay as close as possible to the truth.

"Who is this girl anyway?" Mateo nodded to the flyer. "A sister? Girlfriend?"

"My friend's girlfriend." The man nodded toward the second guy. "He organized a bit of a search party to find her."

The second guy approached the driver's side window and stood next to his friend. Or rather, his cohort.

He eyed Mateo but didn't say anything.

"I hope you have some luck with that." Mateo was anxious to get away from here before these guys asked more questions or maybe even asked to search his vehicle.

After another moment, the first man tapped the

hood of his Jeep. "I'll let you get going. But if you see her, I'd appreciate you letting us know."

"Will do." Mateo offered a nod before pulling away.

It was only after the guys were well in his rearview mirror that he released the breath he held.

That had been close.

And it had left him with more questions than answers.

CHAPTER 24

"You can sit up now."

At the sound of Mateo's voice, relief filled Emily.

She threw the hot blanket from around her and pulled herself upright. She glanced around and saw that the desert surrounded them again.

As she looked back, she saw the gas station was far behind them now.

Carefully, she climbed back into the front seat and slipped her seat belt on.

She wanted to see Mateo's face as she asked him her next few questions. "What was that about?"

He handed her the flyer.

She blanched when she saw her face there. It had been taken off her social media—but it wasn't her professional headshot. No, this was a photo of her taken at Big Sur when she'd gone there with her two sisters. The wind blew her hair, and she had a carefree grin on her face.

That was one of the last times she and her sisters had been together.

Bittersweet memories hit her.

If she'd only known then what she knew now. She would have appreciated those moments more. Treasured them. Scheduled more.

She touched the heart pendant on her necklace—a necklace her older sister had given her.

Then she looked at the flyer again. These guys had chosen the perfect photo to use on the flyer. Emily looked like the all-American girl, the kind who made headlines.

Someone had listed her as a missing person. But they didn't even use her real name. They'd made up a name, Cindy Johnson.

"These guys are willing to go to extreme lengths to find me, aren't they?" Her voice came out just above a whisper.

"They are. They're pretending to do it with good intentions."

"That fits their profile. Like I said, they come across as being noble. But they're not."

"Did you hear that guy's voice?" Mateo asked. "Did you recognize it?"

"It did sound familiar. When I was being held, I could hear several people outside the room talking. But some of them, I never saw their faces."

"This guy was probably six four with a long face and broad shoulders. He doesn't seem to match the description you gave me of Arrow."

"No, he wasn't Arrow. I would have recognized his voice for sure. It didn't sound like Kyle either." She stared at the flyer. "What about this phone number? Do you think we could figure out who it belongs to?"

"I'll ask Charlie to run it, but it's most likely a burner. These guys are too smart to use anything else."

"Of course." Emily let out a defeated sigh.

Mateo's jaw tightened. "We're definitely going to have to be careful. Especially if these guys are being so open and direct about looking for you. This means that people in this area might report seeing you if you're out and about."

Emily crossed her arms, not liking the sound of that. But she couldn't deny the truth in his words.

Mateo was absolutely right.

The stakes just kept getting higher and higher.

———

Mateo didn't like where any of this was going. Didn't like the way those guys had looked so determined. Didn't like the lengths they were going through to find Emily. The only reason they would go through this much trouble was because they felt threatened by her.

They were desperate to stop her from ruining their plan.

He quickly made a call back to Vanishing Ranch to let Charlie know what was going on.

Plus, he asked Charlie if she could get one of her guys out to that gas station. He hadn't been in a position where he could confront those guys himself. But some of the other guys on the team could. They could help to figure out who those men were.

He had memorized their license plate number, and he recited that to Charlie now.

But he was liking this situation less and less all the time.

He could tell it was beginning to wear on Emily also.

She stared out the window now, a forlorn look in her eyes.

"Do you think these guys will have people waiting at my parents' house? That they could be watching for me?"

"It's hard to say," he said. "But we'll be on guard.

At the first sign of anything suspicious, we'll make other plans."

"I can't stop thinking about the idea that they may have gotten to my parents already."

"Let's stay positive," he said. "But at some point, we may have to get the FBI involved. I know that the men threatened you and said that if you got any law enforcement involved there would be steep consequences. And we can only imagine what that might mean. But right now, we really need to play this by ear."

Emily stared out the window again and nodded.

She was going to have to start making some tough decisions . . . and Mateo knew how difficult they were going to be.

CHAPTER 25

Emily felt a rush of nerves as she and Mateo pulled in front of her parents' place a few hours later.

It was a modest ranch-style red-brick house in a suburb of LA. She'd always appreciated her parents' humility, despite what was seen by many as tremendous success.

Her father pastored one of the largest churches on the West Coast. He did it with integrity, avoiding any scandals over his decades of ministry.

Her parents were the best people she knew, people who truly loved God.

Emily never had any doubts about that.

This was the house where she'd grown up, along with her older sister, Trina, and her younger sister,

Libby. Christmases had been spent here. Bible studies. Birthday parties.

Everything.

The place was a safe haven, a place that held so many treasured memories.

"You've got this," Mateo muttered as they stood on the porch with a light breeze ruffling their hair.

Emily started to knock at the door. She would normally just barge right inside, but that didn't feel appropriate right now.

Before her fist connected with the wood, the door flew open.

Her dad stood there.

He was a giant of a man—physically and spiritually. Standing at six foot four, he had broad shoulders, a square face, and gray hair.

He'd always been Emily's rock.

In the blink of an eye, he pulled her into his arms, a guttural cry escaping. A moment later, her mom joined, and the three of them stood on the porch sobbing together.

Emily was *so* glad to see them.

So glad that Mateo gave them a moment.

Finally, the three of them pulled away. When they did, her dad's gaze went to Mateo. He stared at him skeptically, his gaze stopping at the gun holstered to Mateo's side.

Her dad bristled. "Who is this?"

Emily hadn't intended to, but she touched Mateo's arm. She thought he might flinch, but he didn't.

"Dad, this is Mateo. He's a good guy. He . . ." What should she say? She decided to go with the truth. "He rescued me, and he's helping me."

"Rescued you?" Her mom's voice cracked as her eyes welled with tears again.

Emily rubbed her throat, which suddenly felt so tight she could hardly breathe. "We need to talk."

"Yes, we do. A lot has happened, Emily." Her father's voice fell as if defeated.

She tensed. It wasn't something Emily often heard in her father's voice. "What happened? What's wrong?"

His kind but grief-stricken gaze met hers. "We have so much to talk about. So much. Come sit down. Tell us what's going on with you first."

———

Mateo listened as Emily told her parents about what happened.

Everything.

The three of them cried more and hugged each other again.

Their bond was clear, and it was touching.

He gave them space to do what they needed, all while keeping watch near the front window. He wished that Emily had been comfortable enough to let him bring someone else with him. But she'd wanted it to just be the two of them, and he understood her reasoning.

Besides, sometimes it was easier in these operations to keep things simple.

He glanced at Emily's mom. The woman was probably in her early sixties. She had petite features and dark, curly hair that was sprinkled with gray. Emily clearly took after her—both in looks and demeanor.

"Things have been bad here as well," her mom started with a strained voice.

Mateo's spine tightened at her words.

What did that mean? He had a feeling there was more to this story.

"What happened?" Emily clutched her mother's hand.

"Someone sent us a picture of you. You were gagged and tied to a chair. I saw the bruises on your face." Her mom's voice cracked, and another sob escaped, but she quickly covered her mouth. "The note said we'd get further instructions and that if we told the police or anyone else, you'd die."

Mateo stepped closer. "Did you tell the police?"

Emily's father shook his head, a somber look in his gaze. "We didn't know what to do."

"So the police don't know?" Mateo clarified. "No one does?"

"No . . ." Her father rubbed his eyes with an index finger, agony on his features. "Gloria and I talked, and we decided if we didn't hear from anyone by yesterday afternoon, we were going to go to the FBI. But . . ."

Emily stiffened. "But what?"

Her mom's gaze locked on Emily's. "Then they took your little sister."

CHAPTER 26

Emily's world crashed around her.

These men had taken Libby?

How was that even possible? Emily grasped the arm of her chair, needing something to ground her before she slipped into panic.

Mateo touched her elbow. "Maybe I should get you some water."

"It's in the kitchen right behind us," Emily's mom said.

Mateo disappeared through the doorway.

As he did, Emily stared at her mother. Her thoughts still raced as she tried to make sense of the revelation.

Libby was a sophomore at UCLA studying business management.

And she was stunning.

The exact kind of girl that these guys might want to get their hands on—and the right age as well.

"What happened, Mom?"

"They sent us a picture of Libby, just as they did with you." Her mother's voice wavered with grief. "She was also beaten up."

Mateo stepped back into the room, a glass of water in his hand—a glass that seemed nearly forgotten in light of their conversation. "And you still didn't get the police involved?"

Emily's mom and dad glanced at each other.

"Not yet. We didn't know what to do." Her mom burst into tears again and fell into her father's arms.

Emily couldn't stand to see her parents' grief. They didn't deserve this. No one did.

She jumped to her feet, her gaze hard with determination.

Then she announced, "I'm going to find Libby if it's the last thing I do."

———

Mateo sucked in a breath when he heard Emily's words.

Just how exactly was she planning to find her

sister? Operations like that . . . they were complicated. Involved manpower. Detailed research. Self-defense skills.

In other words, trained professionals with resources.

Her parents stared at Emily, their foreheads wrinkled and their eyes narrowed with concern.

"Emily . . . after what you've been through, you need to take time to heal." Her father's voice sounded gentle but firm.

"There's no way I'm going to sit back and not do anything." Fire flared in Emily's eyes. "Not if I have the means to help."

"Emily . . ." Her mother's voice trailed with worry. "That's a bad idea. We can't lose both of you . . ."

Mateo knew Emily well enough to know she wasn't going to back down.

He also knew he couldn't send her out there alone to fight this battle.

He stepped forward. "Respectfully, I work with the best of the best. We'd like to help."

Her father eyed him again. "And who are you exactly?"

"I'm a former Mexican federal police officer. I now work for an organization that helps people in desperate situations. We have former SEALs, FBI, and CIA on our team."

Her father still looked unconvinced. "Why haven't I ever heard of your organization before?"

"Because privacy is our weapon. It's how we keep people safe."

Her father seemed to think about those words a moment before nodding. "At this point, I'm desperate. I'll take any help I can get. But I prefer Emily not be involved. We thought we'd lost her. And we have another daughter missing now. I can't go through that again." His voice broke, and he bent forward as sobs wracked his body.

"We'll keep Emily safe," Mateo said.

After a few moments, Pastor Holcomb pulled himself together and straightened, unapologetically studying Mateo. "Are you a Bible-believing man?"

"Yes, sir. I am. My boss doesn't hire anyone who isn't."

"Then I can assume you're a man of your word."

"I am."

Pastor Holcomb stared at him another moment before standing and offering an affirmative nod. "Okay then. Find Libby. And keep our Emily safe. Please." He held out a hand to Mateo.

Mateo shook hands with Emily's father as he took

those words to heart. It was the same admonishment that Rose's parents had given him.

And he'd failed.

Mateo had vowed he would never let that happen again.

CHAPTER 27

Emily hugged her parents before she and Mateo hit the road.

As to be expected, it was a tearful goodbye.

Part of her wanted to go upstairs to her old room and curl into her childhood bed and pretend like none of this had happened.

But those men had her sister. Emily meant it when she said she would do everything within her power to find Libby.

Her mom had packed them some food and water for the road. That was her mom for you. She was always thinking of others.

But it was smart to take food with them rather than risk hitting a drive-thru or other detour. Plus, her mom had made her famous chicken salad sandwiches. It was Emily's favorite and a small blessing on an otherwise dismal day.

As she and Mateo climbed into the Jeep, Emily noticed Mateo glancing around.

Realization filled her.

"Do you think we're being watched right now?" Her heart pounded harder.

"I have no idea. But I have to be cautious, just in case."

"Of course." Emily shuddered. So much danger seemed to surround them.

Emily had been a Christian for a long time. For as long as she could remember, she had sung "Jesus Loves Me" and had gone to church and known in her heart that God was real.

But she'd never been able to understand why God allowed so much cruelty to happen to some people while other people skated by. The fact that Emily had been abducted and now her sister . . . it was too much.

She'd finally realized there was no good answer to that question. She simply had to let it go and trust that God had a plan.

But at times like these, that trust was hard. More than hard.

It was the most agonizing thing she'd ever had to do.

As Mateo started down the road, Emily let out a breath. She didn't see anyone suspicious around them.

Maybe they were safe.

For now, at least.

Her relief didn't last long as her thoughts turned to her sister again.

"What now? How are we going to find Libby? Mateo, she's my little sister, and she's the sweetest person in the whole world. She wants to be a missionary. Now these guys have her." Emily covered her mouth before another cry could escape.

But there was no use.

The sob came anyway.

Mateo stole a glance at her and frowned compassionately. "We need to figure out who took you and where you were being held."

"Can we track down any information on the cell phone number connected with those text messages my parents received?" Emily asked.

"We can try. But it's doubtful we'll discover anything that way. These guys are too good for that, and I'm sure they used a burner. But I promise we'll utilize every resource necessary in order to find her."

"Thank you. And I'll do whatever I can to help. No matter how painful the memories might be, I'll do whatever I have to." Determination edged her voice.

"I know you will."

Her thoughts remained on Libby and what her sister might be going through right now. Each scenario seemed to get worse and worse.

"Oh, Mateo . . . Libby could be out of the country by now." She rubbed a hand over her face. "What if I hadn't escaped at all? Would that mean they wouldn't have grabbed my sister?"

Emily's voice trembled as emotion welled inside her.

Mateo squeezed her arm. "You can't think like that."

Her gaze met his. "How can I not?"

Before he could answer, Mateo glanced in the rearview mirror and stiffened.

"What is it?" Emily asked.

"I think we're being followed."

———

Mateo glanced in his rearview mirror again, keeping his eye on the car behind them.

"Do you think someone was watching my parents' house, and we just didn't see them?" Emily asked.

Mateo gripped the steering wheel. "I don't know. I tried to keep an eye on the area, and I didn't see anything. But that doesn't mean they weren't there."

Emily leaned closer. "We can't let them catch us."

"I won't." He meant the words. If those guys tracked them down and got Emily, he would probably never see her again.

Just like he hadn't seen Rose again.

That outcome wasn't an option.

He pressed the accelerator harder.

Right now, they were still in the suburbs of LA, where traffic was heavy and thick.

That also gave them plenty of chances to get away.

Out in the desert where it was just an open stretch of road, there was nowhere to hide.

The last thing he wanted to do was to lead whoever was following them to Vanishing Ranch. That also meant that he would need to take a different way back this time.

He would figure that out later. For now, he needed to try and lose them.

"You're going to need to hold on," Mateo said.

Before she could respond, he took a sharp left into traffic.

Cars honked around him, but he ignored them.

Right now, keeping everyone safe was his priority. Mateo couldn't be careless. He couldn't put the lives of other drivers in danger.

But he had to lose this guy.

And he had an idea of just how to do that.

He took another quick turn—right this time.

As he did, he ducked into a nearby parking garage.

"A parking garage?" Emily looked at him with wide eyes. "Isn't this just like a dead end?"

"Trust me." He quickly whipped his Jeep around, remaining on the ground level. But he pulled behind the gate, near a wall that would block them from sight.

This should give them an advantage.

With any luck, the other driver would think that he had turned at the next corner.

This would buy them the time that they needed.

He hoped.

He glanced through a small crack in the parking garage wall, waiting to see the other vehicle—a dark colored sedan—go by.

Finally, he spotted it.

Just as he'd hoped, the vehicle made the next right-hand turn.

He would give it a few minutes, and then he would backtrack the way they'd come.

And then he'd find an alternate route back to Vanishing Ranch.

He glanced at Emily. "You okay?"

Her limbs were trembling, but she nodded.

He wished he could do something to comfort her, but he couldn't. Especially not right now.

Finally, enough time passed.

He slowly crept forward.

But he knew there was a good chance this wasn't over yet.

CHAPTER 28

Emily was quiet as they continued the drive back to Vanishing Ranch. She didn't have the desire to talk. Mostly, she just thought about Libby.

Libby . . . who literally gave her coat to a homeless man once. Who was homecoming queen even though she didn't care a lick about being popular. Who started a student-led Bible study in high school that grew to more than fifty people.

She was one of a kind.

And she didn't deserve what she was going through right now.

Emily covered her mouth before another cry could escape.

Mateo shifted in the driver's seat as he looked at her. "I'm sorry you're going through this, Emily."

"Thank you."

He started to say something else when his phone rang.

It was Charlie. Mateo answered through the Jeep's hands-free system and gave her the update.

"I'm glad you're both okay," Charlie said. "Emily, we'll help you find your sister. I promise."

She rubbed her throat as emotion burned there. "Thank you."

"In the meantime, I have an update for you as well. I've been looking into this Arrow guy."

Emily straightened. "Did you figure out his real name?"

"Not yet, unfortunately. But Mateo . . . Miguel Sanchez, the leader of the Gemini Cartel, was killed during a shootout with the police after your wife's murder, correct?"

His jaw visibly tightened. "That's right. I was the one who shot him. He was the puppet master who pulled all the strings. He had the charity leadership under his thumb."

"It turns out he has a son named Diego—most people don't know this," Charlie said. "I guess Diego's mom was Miguel's secret girlfriend. Anyway, rumor has it that Diego has taken over and the cartel has regrouped."

"Doesn't surprise me," Mateo muttered.

"We're wondering if this Arrow guy is actually Diego. Maybe he's even trying to get payback since you killed his father. We're trying to find a photo of him. You didn't by chance go to the academy with someone with that name, did you?"

"Not that I remember. But . . . there was one guy who dropped out early. He committed some type of infraction, and they sent him home."

"Let's see if we can find out his name. We'll keep researching. But I just wanted to let you know what we learned."

"Thanks." Mateo hit the End button on his screen.

Emily pointed to something up ahead and grabbed Mateo's arm. "Do you see that?"

He hit the brakes slightly. "Lights."

"Do you think . . ." Her voice trailed. She wasn't sure if her question would make her sound unreasonable.

"That it's someone looking for you?"

"I mean . . . there's nothing else out here but the ranch."

"We've been trying to track down those lights in the desert. Maybe these are the same guys." Mateo cut his headlights and pulled to the side of the road. "Maybe they're the ones who buried that body out there. They could even be burying someone else. That's what I need to find out."

————

Mateo turned to Emily. "Stay here."

"You're leaving me in the Jeep?"

"It's safer here." He pressed his gun into her hands. "Use this if you have to."

"But . . ."

"Be careful. There's a bullet in the chamber." He gave her a quick lesson on how to release the safety and pull the trigger if necessary.

"Now I need to go see who's out there. This could be our chance to get some answers."

She stared at him another moment, her eyes wide. But finally, she nodded.

With one more glance at her, Mateo stepped out and motioned for her to lock the doors behind him.

He waited until she did before taking off on foot toward the lights in the distance.

If he moved fast enough, he should be able to catch up with them.

Should be able to find out some answers.

He hadn't seen anybody on the road behind them, so Emily should be safe.

He continued to close in on the lights.

Just as before, there were three different beams indicating three people were out here.

Most people didn't wander this desert at night. Didn't know what they were getting themselves into.

But these guys obviously had a mission.

Was that to find Emily?

He didn't know.

He paused behind a rock as he got closer, not wanting to be seen. He didn't want to confront these guys directly. First, he wanted to know what they were doing out here. He was most likely to find that out if he didn't ask them directly. At least, that was true if their intentions were as nefarious as he thought they were.

He crouched and waited. As he did, he heard one of the men say, "It will take weeks to search this desert. It's like looking for a needle in a haystack."

"We can't give up," another man said. "If we don't find what we're looking for, we're all dead. You heard what he said—failure's not an option."

Were these men looking for Emily?

It was the only thing that made sense.

Mateo prepared to find out for certain.

CHAPTER 29

Emily's nerves felt ready to snap as she waited.

She really wished she could have gone with Mateo.

But she understood his reasoning for wanting her to stay here.

Still, as she gripped the gun in her hands, she wondered if she would be able to pull this trigger.

She wasn't sure.

Her only hope in the situation was that Mateo truly might get some answers.

But if those guys saw him, they could turn on him.

What if they overpowered Mateo?

Then what would she do?

She grabbed her phone and looked at it.

But she had no signal out here.

She wasn't surprised.

But she did realize just how quickly this situation might go south.

She glanced out the side window and squinted.

Wait . . . was that . . . another light?

It was.

There was somebody else out here, coming from the opposite direction of those other lights that they'd seen.

Alarm raced through her.

If this guy shone his light on the Jeep, it would reflect off the sides of it.

And she would be a sitting duck.

She knew Mateo had said to use the gun if she had to. But that was the last thing she wanted.

But she also didn't want to be found and confronted.

She only had a moment to make her decision.

Finally, she climbed from the Jeep and quietly shut the door.

Then she scrambled around the large rock on the other side and hid.

She still had the gun in her hand, but she would wait and see what this man did before she made any hasty decisions.

As she waited, the flashlight beam hit the rocks around her, and she heard footsteps getting close.

———

Mateo glanced back at where he'd left the Jeep.

That's when he saw another light.

He took one more glance at the shadowed men on the other side of the road.

He wanted to stay.

To see their faces.

To hear more of their conversation.

But he couldn't.

Not if Emily was in danger.

Quietly, he scrambled across the rocky desert terrain.

Headed toward the Jeep.

Where had this other guy even come from? It didn't make any sense.

But he'd figure that out later.

Right now, all he cared about was Emily's safety.

As he got closer, he saw a man peering into his Jeep.

He held his breath.

Was Emily still inside?

Would she shoot?

He didn't want to wait to find out.

He was going to have to plan his next moves carefully.

And time was quickly running out.

———

Emily peeked out from behind the rock and saw a man looking into the Jeep.

She ducked behind the rock again, willing herself to remain quiet.

The man was close. Too close.

Fear seized her as she realized just how dire this situation was. Her lungs tightened, and her heart raced. The gun trembled in her hand.

Even if she had to aim and fire, would she hit her target?

She didn't know.

The thought of firing the gun at a human being made her stomach queasy.

Best-case scenario, the guy wouldn't find her.

Worst case . . . she didn't want to contemplate.

As she shifted to sink lower, a rock beneath her foot rolled.

Emily sucked in a breath, and she froze.

She'd just given herself away, hadn't she?

Please, make me invisible, Emily prayed quietly as she remained as still as possible.

But she heard the footsteps.

They were coming closer.

And closer.

This man could find her.

What would he do with her when he did?

She tried to sink farther behind the rock, but she couldn't. She knew if she tried to find a new place to hide, he would hear her moving. If she tried to run, he'd see her.

She felt trapped.

She prayed she would blend into the shadows.

As the man got closer, a hand pressed over her mouth.

Panic surged through her.

Someone had circled around behind her.

Had Arrow found her again?

CHAPTER 30

Mateo pressed one hand over Emily's mouth and used his other hand to grab the gun from her, all while praying she didn't make a sound.

He had wanted to let her know about his presence. But he knew if he startled her, she might scream—or shoot him.

"It's me," he whispered in her ear. "Mateo."

She stopped squirming, and her shoulders loosened slightly.

"Stay quiet," he murmured.

She nodded and remained still, totally silent.

When he was sure Emily wouldn't react, he lowered his hand from her mouth.

As a protective measure, he slipped an arm around her as he watched the man in the distance.

He crept closer to their spot, muttering beneath his breath as the beam of his flashlight scattered illumination on the ground.

Mateo wasn't sure if this guy would find them here or not.

He would fight the man if he had to.

But Mateo hoped it didn't come down to violence.

As the footsteps paced closer, he realized the likelihood of this turning ugly continued to increase.

Emily trembled beside him but remained quiet.

Finally, the man paused.

He said something into his radio.

And then he turned to leave.

Mateo wanted to release his breath, to feel relieved. But he couldn't.

Not yet.

They needed to remain hidden until he was certain the men were gone and the coast was clear.

He just hoped this man hadn't called in backup.

Emily turned and tucked herself against Mateo as they crouched behind the rocky outcropping.

Thank goodness he'd come looking for her.

She felt much safer having him by her side.

But what had those guys been planning? Were

they trying to find her? Had Arrow sent them?

That made the most sense.

Finally, after the men were gone, Mateo removed his arm from around her and stood.

Between his muscular biceps, his tattooed arms, and his dark, curly hair that fell into his eyes, he was a sight to behold. Part of her wanted to reach forward. To bring him back closer to her.

But she couldn't do that.

Even if she wanted to.

She *really* wanted to.

Finally, Mateo nodded. "I need to get you back."

"What about those guys?" She stood and nodded in the distance where the men had been.

"They're all probably long gone by now." Mateo took her arm and led her over the rocky terrain toward the Jeep.

"Did you hear them say anything when you approached them?" she finally asked.

His gaze darkened. "Just that they're looking for something—or someone."

"Did you see their faces?"

"Unfortunately, no. It was too dark."

The rest of the ride back to the ranch was quiet.

Too quiet.

But it wasn't for a lack of things to talk about.

It was because they both felt danger closing in.

CHAPTER 31

Emily had another restless night. She couldn't stop thinking about Libby. Where she was. If she was injured. How these guys might have hurt her.

Finally, at the crack of dawn, Emily had arisen and dressed. She pulled on an Arizona Cardinals sweatshirt as she stepped outside, the air chillier than usual.

She paused near her door, and her gaze wandered the ranch.

She knew exactly who she was looking for.

Mateo.

How was it that the man had made such an impression on her? Maybe it was because he'd saved her life more than once.

That could do it to a person.

But she was intrigued by him. By his story. She wanted to know more.

And that fact scared her.

Especially after Kyle. She'd had the wool pulled over her eyes so easily that it made her question her judgment.

Would she ever be able to truly trust a man again?

She didn't know, but if she did . . . Mateo would be the one.

She shoved those thoughts aside for now.

Instead, she walked toward the mess hall thinking she'd grab some coffee and visit with Chef a few minutes while he prepared breakfast.

But, to her surprise, several people were already inside eating a savory breakfast of eggs and bacon.

Charlie and Monroe were at a table finishing up their meal. Charlie stood when Emily walked in and motioned her over.

"Why don't you grab some food and then we can go to my office?" Charlie asked.

Emily didn't argue.

Maybe Charlie had an update for her.

She grabbed a plate and some coffee before following Charlie and Monroe.

Mateo was already settled in Charlie's office, and he stood and pulled out a chair for Emily when he spotted her.

Emily's heart sped at the sight of him, which was silly.

These feelings were the last thing she needed right now.

As she sat next to Mateo, she focused on sipping her coffee and balancing her plate in her lap.

"All right." Charlie sat in her chair, her razor-sharp gaze focusing on the task at hand. "Here's what we know. Tucker—your former bodyguard—has gone radio silent. No one has seen or heard from him in a week."

Emily frowned. He'd been involved, hadn't he?

She immediately began to lose her appetite and set the plate of food on the side of Charlie's desk.

"Those men at the gas station who were handing out flyers?" Charlie continued. "They were gone by the time we got there. We ran their plates, but their car was apparently stolen a few days ago in Vegas."

Another dead end.

"The dead man Mateo found?" Charlie said. "Apparently, the sheriff hasn't been able to identify him yet."

"What about that guy who left the academy?" Mateo asked. "Did you have a chance to look into him?"

"He died in a car accident three years ago. He's not behind this."

Emily frowned. She'd hoped for answers, but that didn't appear to be what she would get today.

"And Diego?" Mateo shifted, his eyes narrowed with thought. "Did you find out if he was involved in this? Or if, in fact, he is Arrow?"

"I have guys out there gathering information. We feel confident he's involved. But we're still waiting to hear more."

Emily leaned back, wishing she had more to go on. "So, what do I do now? Sit back and wait for these guys to send me instructions on how to find my sister?"

"If you want to know what I think—" Mateo started.

Before he could finish the sentence, a crash sounded in the distance.

Charlie, Mateo, and Emily jumped up and headed toward the mess hall.

But everyone in the room was already on their way outside.

————

Mateo sprinted outside.

Had someone found them?

Was this an attack?

He paused in the courtyard, several others behind him.

That's when he saw two women, standing outside one of the guest cottages, clinging to each other as they stared at the roof.

He ran toward them, urgency pumping through his veins. "Is everything okay?"

The two women shook their heads.

"No . . . something crashed through the roof." One of the women pointed to the cottage.

Mateo darted into the building, still thinking in worst-case scenarios. Bombing. Attacks. Sabotage.

But, when he stepped inside, he saw the rock on the floor.

No, not a normal rock.

It was probably eight inches by four with all the qualities of a rock—however, it was black and shiny. And a strange, metallic scent surrounded it.

As he reached to touch it, he jerked his hand back. Intense heat emanated from the object.

Was that a . . . ?

Mateo stepped closer and kicked it.

This was definitely *not* an ordinary rock.

If he wasn't mistaken—and based on the molten ash sides—this was a meteorite.

Charlie and Monroe joined him, pausing on either side of him.

"What *is* that?" Charlie asked as she stared at the object.

Monroe stepped closer. "Good question."

"I think it's a meteorite," Mateo said, realizing how foolish he might sound.

Charlie looked up at him, not bothering to hide the skepticism in her gaze. "Really?"

He nodded at the hole in the ceiling. "It apparently came from the sky."

"I mean . . . what are the odds?" Charlie muttered with a quick shrug as she continued to stare at it.

"Just be glad no one got hurt." Monroe rubbed his jaw as if perplexed by the situation also.

"Oh, I am," Charlie said. "But strange things happen sometimes in the desert, don't they?"

Mateo raised his eyebrows. "You can say that again."

Mateo had his fill of strange, enough to last him a lifetime.

CHAPTER 32

As the Vanishing Ranch staff investigated the meteorite, Emily escaped to her guest cottage.

She needed to find out more information about her sister, and she didn't have any time to waste.

For that reason, she sat on the edge of her bed and began calling Libby's friends.

The last time they'd seen her was two days ago. Libby had been walking to the campus library to study. Then she'd mysteriously disappeared.

Just what had those men done to her?

Anger burned through Emily's blood at the thought of it.

Everything seemed to be taking place too slowly. She didn't want to sound ungrateful for the help everyone here at the ranch had offered. Nor did she want to be impatient.

But every second counted right now. She almost would feel better if she was out there wandering the wilderness. At least, she would be doing *something*.

After she called the last person on her list, she lowered her phone and sighed.

She really didn't know anything new now—and she definitely didn't know anything that would help her find Libby.

She needed to figure out what to do next.

But first she would find Mateo.

———

After lunch, Mateo decided to head to town.

Emily had convinced him to let her tag along.

He knew every time she left the ranch, she was at risk. But he could understand her insistence to help find her sister.

To help conceal her identity, she'd donned a cowboy hat and wig. Hopefully no one would recognize her.

They headed to the closest town—which just happened to be more than thirty miles away. There wasn't much to the municipality—just a grocery store, a gas station, and a small bar. A few other buildings housed a pottery studio and a salvage store.

Mateo had changed into some ripped jeans, a baseball cap, and a Patagonia T-shirt. He hoped to look like a tourist passing through instead of a former federal law enforcement officer.

This watering hole was where locals liked to shoot the breeze.

He wanted to know if other people had seen anything strange in the desert lately.

He and Emily walked into the dark, hole-in-the-wall establishment. Just as Mateo had expected, the interior was grimy, with outdated furnishings, and it smelled like body odor and beer.

Bars weren't his scene. But maybe he could find out some information here.

"Keep your head low," he whispered to Emily as they walked through the doorway. "We can't draw any attention."

She nodded, but her gaze showed her apprehension.

The two of them sat at the bar and ordered drinks.

Then Mateo listened to the scuttlebutt around him.

Everyone seemed to be talking about the meteorites. Apparently, the rocks hadn't just fallen on Vanishing Ranch, but several had fallen throughout the area over the past month. It had some people nervous, and others fascinated.

"It's because of the lizard people," said a fiftyish woman with bright red hair and a full face, who sat two seats down.

Mateo tried not to show any surprise. "Lizard people?"

Mateo knew lizard people didn't exist. But this whole situation was getting weirder and weirder.

"I saw them running around at night near my dad's ranch," the bartender said. "They only come out at night."

Several other people piped in with their agreement.

He and Emily exchanged a glance.

As people continued telling their stories, the guy on the other side of Mateo turned toward him and shook his head. "I love hearing people talk about this area."

The guy wore a trucker hat, had a beer belly, and his black-and-white beard came halfway down his chest. Mateo could tell by the man's tone and friendly gaze that he was a talker, maybe even a storyteller.

Just the kind of person Mateo needed to chat with.

"It's definitely interesting around here," Mateo

agreed. "My girlfriend and I are just passing through, but I'm fascinated."

The man nodded a greeting to Emily.

She nodded back before lowering her head.

"You should be fascinated," the man continued.

Mateo leaned back, trying to remain casual. "What's this area like? Mostly just people wanting to be off the grid and left alone? The artistic types?"

"We have a lot of those. But sometimes you find people who don't fit that mold."

Mateo shifted again, careful to keep his voice even. "Yeah, like I saw this house built into the side of the mountain probably about ten miles from here. I've been fascinated by it ever since. Never seen anything like it before. What's the story behind it?"

The guy raised his eyebrows, and his eyes lit. "Well, it's funny that you asked."

CHAPTER 33

Emily tried to keep her expression even, to not show any signs of excitement.

But was this the information they were looking for?

"What can you tell me?" Mateo glanced at the man beside him.

"The place went up for sale a while back. I heard some eccentric guy bought it, but he doesn't come around very often. Mostly, his wife uses it."

"That surprises me. I'm surprised a woman—no offense to women—" Mateo shot a withering glance Emily's way. "That a woman would want to stay at a place like that by herself. It's in the middle of nowhere."

The man shrugged. "I heard she's some kind of Mexican royalty."

Emily sucked in a breath. Mexican royalty?

Was that the connection they were looking for?

Had the owner of that house married into the cartel?

It seemed like a good possibility.

Things kept going back to that house.

Emily stored away each new fact.

That property definitely appeared to be tied to some of the issues they'd been dealing with.

They needed to let Charlie know. Right now, she was supposed to be working on figuring out how people were getting in and out of that house. If there was a secret entrance, that would make it the perfect place to traffic people, or drugs, or illegal firearms, or all of the above.

There were too many things happening.

Meteorites?

Lizard people?

And the most serious of all . . . Libby was missing.

A frown tugged at her lips.

"Why is the house built into the side of the mountain?" Mateo continued. "Any story behind that?"

The man shrugged. "I'm not sure. You want that information, talk to John Quito."

"Who's John Quito?" Mateo asked.

"He lives about an hour from here. He's a bit of an expert in all things desert. He and his family have been around forever, and his wife sells real estate. Maybe she even sold that house. I'm not sure."

John Quito sounded exactly like someone they needed to talk to.

After a few more minutes, Mateo paid their bill and then they headed to his Jeep.

———

As soon as they were back in the Jeep, Emily turned to him. "We've got to talk to this John guy."

That was exactly what Mateo had expected her to say. Still, his shoulders tensed. "I don't know if that's a good idea while you're with me."

Her gaze pleaded with him. "Please. I need to know. Plus, think of all the time you'll waste taking me back first."

Mateo raked a hand through his hair as he tried to think this through. "I need to run this past the team."

"We don't have much time. Every second counts."

He couldn't make any hasty decisions, not when so much was on the line.

He also had to consider Emily's safety.

His gaze locked with hers. "I should go alone."

Emily's determined gaze latched onto his. "I can't stay at the ranch and not do anything while my sister is out there."

"We don't know what we're going to be getting ourselves into, however." Mateo lowered his voice as concern rushed through him. "You don't want to put yourself in a situation where these guys can grab you again."

"I know. Believe me, I know. But I have to do *something*."

Mateo still wasn't sure it was a good idea. In fact, he *knew* this wasn't a good idea. But the last thing he wanted was to hold Emily at the ranch as if she were imprisoned. Besides, knowing Emily, she'd try to go on her own to investigate.

He finally nodded with resignation. "Okay. But you need to listen to me."

"I will."

Every time they went out, it was a risk.

So far, they'd dodged trouble . . . for the most part.

But how long would that be the case?

CHAPTER 34

An hour later, they pulled up to John's place. Just as the stranger at the bar had said, it was located about an hour away from the watering hole.

Emily felt her nerves thrum through her as she anticipated what she might—or might not—learn.

John's house wasn't fancy—just a little cinderblock home that had been painted pink. The outside was neat, despite all the lawn ornaments in the front yard. There were flamingos with spinning wings, bicycles with bright wheels, and even a canvas dog that turned in circles.

As they stepped from the Jeep, the sounds of the spinners filled the air, adding a creepy vibe to the area.

She almost changed her mind.

But she couldn't. Not since they'd come this far.

Mateo turned to Emily. "We've got our cover story."

She nodded. Mateo was posing as a journalist, and she was his girlfriend, who just happened to be traveling with him as he did a set of articles on small Southwest towns.

Mateo leaned closer. "It's not too late to change your mind."

Emily squared her shoulders, regretting that he must have seen her fear. "I have to know."

Still staring at her, he nodded slowly. "Very well then. Let's do this."

As soon as they stepped toward the house, the front door opened. A slight man with leathery skin and a fedora stepped out.

But it was the gun in his hands that made Emily freeze.

"Can I help you?" the man yelled.

Mateo raised his hands, still calm and cool. "We don't mean any harm. We just have a few questions for you."

The man narrowed his eyes. "What kind of questions?"

"I'm a journalist doing an article about this area of the country. I was told you're an expert."

"Oh, yeah? Who told you that?"

"Someone at the watering hole," Mateo said.

The man—John Quito, she assumed—still eyed them suspiciously.

Emily held her breath.

What would he do next?

Her gaze went to his gun.

His finger was on the trigger, even though the barrel pointed toward their feet.

Still, her heart thrummed as she waited to find out if he would help or not.

———

Mateo didn't like how this visit was going so far.

He would be quicker on the draw than this man.

But he hated that Emily could be in the crossfire.

John lowered his gun, but his expression remained aloof. "I guess I could answer a few questions."

Mateo released his breath—but not completely.

The situation was still sticky.

John crossed his arms. "What do you want to know?"

Mateo edged closer, careful that Emily remained behind him. "I'm curious about the history of that house that's built into the side of the mountain about an hour from here."

John's eyes lit with familiarity. "I'm aware of it. My wife is the one who sold it. What do you want to know about it?"

"What's the story behind it?" Mateo asked. "It seems so interesting."

"It was built during the Cold War. The man who built it made millions in the oil business, so no expense was spared."

"I heard it might have tunnels running into it. Hidden tunnels." Mateo paused, hoping this guy would take the bait.

John's eyebrows flickered up. "You heard that, huh?"

"That's right. Is it true?"

John eyed them again. "Depends on why you want to know. I'm not sure the property owner would appreciate having a detail like that published, especially if the point is privacy." He raised his gun again. "Now, why don't you tell me why you're really here?"

CHAPTER 35

Emily sucked in a breath.

What if this guy was in on this whole scheme—whatever scheme that might be? She and Mateo could have just walked into a trap.

"There's no need to aim that gun at us." Mateo's voice remained steady.

"Then start talking. People don't come around asking about that house for no reason." The words came out sharp and biting.

Emily waited to see what Mateo's next move would be. In the meantime, she didn't dare move.

"Okay, the truth is I'm not a journalist," Mateo finally said.

"I had a feeling. Go on." John narrowed his eyes.

"Her sister is missing, and we fear she might be

being kept there," Mateo said. "That's the truth. We're trying to find out more information."

John held his gun steady.

Emily's lungs remained frozen as she waited.

Finally, he lowered his gun again.

His gaze—and stature—seemed to soften.

"Tell me what you need to know," John said. "I'd be happy to help in whatever way I can."

Emily's heart continued to pound in her ears. Did this man have information they needed?

She prayed he did.

Because they were running out of time.

Libby was running out of time.

———

"Yes, there are tunnels that lead into the house," John said as they sat in his house with some freshly squeezed lemonade in front of them. "The original owner eventually got into the drug trade, and he needed a way of transporting them without being seen. My impression is that the openings are on the other side of the mountain."

As Mateo processed what John said, he took another sip of his drink.

Now that the man was warming up, he was chatty. Very chatty.

But their chatting was taking too much time.

"So, these tunnels are easy to find?" Mateo clarified.

"I wouldn't say they're *easy*. But if you look hard enough, you should be able to find them."

Mateo nodded, soaking in every detail. "You know anything about the new owner?"

"I heard his wife is mixed up in some things. I've heard rumors that trucks have been seen heading that direction at night. Otherwise, the two of them pretty much keep to themselves."

"What kind of things is his wife mixed up with?" Emily leaned closer.

"I'm not sure. Maybe the cartel. You can only imagine what kind of things the cartel does. Drugs, human trafficking, money laundering. Take your pick." John paused and looked at Emily. "If your sister is with them, then you need to find her."

Emily rubbed her neck. "I know."

He leaned closer. "If you want to get to meet the owners of that house, I might have a way you can do that."

"What's that?"

"There's a fundraiser coming up. Not far from here."

"When is this fundraiser?" Mateo asked.

"Tomorrow night. I heard there are a couple of tickets left."

CHAPTER 36

Mateo and Emily left two hours later.

Once John had warmed up to them, he'd been very forthcoming. They'd talked about the party and had gathered more information. Then John had talked about desert birds, plants, monsoons, and anything else he could think about.

Mateo's mind raced through everything he'd learned, sorting out the important information from the trivial.

He had to think of a way to attend that fundraiser.

But at the moment, all he wanted was to get Emily back to the ranch. Out here on the road at night, it seemed too exposed. He could practically feel the danger crackling in the air around them.

They headed down the lonely highway back toward the ranch.

In the dark, it was hard to see anything except the road in front of them.

The only good part about being out here in the open was that he could see anyone coming or going.

"I'm so worried about Libby," Emily murmured as she leaned back in her seat.

Mateo reached over and squeezed her hand, sensing she needed comfort. He wished he could offer more than words. But he tried to maintain his distance, despite his growing attraction.

"We're doing everything we can to find her," he finally said, his voice sounding hoarse.

"I know." Emily muttered as apprehension filled her gaze. "This is all such a nightmare."

Mateo had seen his fair share of nightmares. He'd even lived through many. He knew about the pain they involved. He didn't wish that on anyone.

But maybe that fundraising party would hold some answers.

Something about Emily reminded him of Rose. Maybe it was the hint of stubborn determination. Maybe it was the fact that she was frightened but there was still strength behind her gaze.

He wasn't sure.

But the comparison brought him a wave of bitter-sweetness.

Every day, he missed Rose. He missed her soft touch, easy smile, nurturing spirit.

And every day, Mateo regretted he hadn't been able to save her.

She'd been the bravest, most giving person he'd ever known. She'd even turned down high-paying jobs in order to work with a nonprofit that helped feed hungry children in their town.

He would have never guessed that very same giving spirit would be what ultimately led to her death.

He squinted as something appeared on the road ahead.

It almost looked like a . . . box.

A box?

What sense did that make?

Mateo slowed, assuming something had fallen out of someone's vehicle.

But as he got closer, he saw two small lights blinking on top.

He sucked in a breath.

"Hold on!" He jerked the wheel to the right.

As he did, an explosion filled the air.

Someone had known Mateo and Emily were coming this way.

They'd left an explosive in their path.

Mateo's thoughts became fuzzy as the Jeep tumbled, and tumbled, and tumbled.

———

Emily's world spun around her.

Her ears rang as she squinted, trying to let her thoughts catch up to reality.

What just happened?

At once, she remembered the explosion.

Someone had put a bomb in the road.

They'd rolled several times.

At least, the Jeep had landed upright.

But fear pulsed through her as she saw flames shooting up from the hood.

There was another scent also.

Was that . . . gas?

Emily sucked in a breath.

This whole vehicle just might go up in flames.

Ignoring the ache in her head, Emily glanced over.

Mateo . . .

Blood gushed from his forehead, and his eyes were closed as he lay there unmoving.

Panic raced through her.

Was he alive?

She grabbed his arm and shook him. "Mateo . . . Mateo!"

He didn't stir.

She glanced behind her.

If someone had triggered that bomb to go off when it did, that probably meant they were most likely in the nearby hills watching them.

They might even try to get to them now.

She and Mateo needed to run.

Now.

There was no way she was leaving Mateo behind.

"You've got to wake up," she muttered as she shook him again.

He moaned and finally stirred—but just slightly.

Relief rushed through her. At least, he was alive.

"Mateo . . ." Emily said louder this time.

His eyes fluttered open. He blinked. Then he looked at her.

"Emily . . . are you okay?" His voice sounded throaty.

"Yes, but we have to get out of here. Now."

She pressed his seat belt button, and it released. Then she did the same for herself.

She scrambled from the Jeep, all too aware that a bullet could fly her way at any minute. Her heart stammered out of control at the thought.

She ran around the front of the vehicle. But when

she reached Mateo's door, she saw the metal had crumbled like an accordion.

There was no way she could get that open.

A whiff of gas swirled around her, reminding her of the urgency of the situation.

She ran back to her side and reached inside. "You need to come this way, Mateo. Hurry. I can smell the gas in the air."

Mateo nodded, his eyes still dazed.

He moved—slowly, but at least he was moving.

As soon as he scooted over the center console, Emily reached under his arms and tugged him the rest of the way out. He tumbled onto the ground before finally pulling himself to his feet.

Emily glanced at the ground and saw a red dot of light there.

She sucked in a breath.

A red light from a gun scope.

They had even less time than she thought.

CHAPTER 37

ateo tried to control his thoughts, his mind.

But his head spun.

His shoulder hurt.

Blood dripped from his temple.

"Mateo . . ." Emily gasped, her eyes wide and filled with concern.

The next instant, she slipped her arm around his waist to hold him up.

Bullets began firing from behind them, hitting the ground around them with soft thuds.

He and Emily lumbered away just as another explosion filled the air.

The Jeep.

They tumbled to the ground, holding each other.

Heat singed the hair on his arm.

Emily gasped but pulled herself to her feet as her survival instincts seemed to kick in.

The sound of the explosion had caused a burst of adrenaline. The fuzziness instantly cleared from Mateo's head.

He righted himself as his heart pumped harder. "Come on. We've got to keep moving."

He took Emily's hand and began pulling her farther away from the Jeep.

Men were obviously hiding in the mountains.

That meant he and Emily had to find shelter. Otherwise, they'd be sitting ducks.

Out here, there wasn't much to block them from the bullets.

For now, distance would be their friend.

Just then, something hit the ground beside them.

Another bullet.

Emily gasped.

Mateo pulled her through the dark desert, running in a zigzag pattern as more bullets sprayed the ground around them.

Soon, they'd be out of range of the gunman. He felt certain the shooter had positioned himself in the hills.

He and Emily just had to keep moving.

But, with every step, Mateo found himself growing wearier.

He touched his shoulder and felt the moisture there. A large gash cut through his shirt and into his skin.

He was losing a lot of blood.

But he couldn't stop until he knew Emily was safe.

———

Emily tried to remain calm, even though the situation felt hopeless.

She had to believe she and Mateo could get out of this trap.

But she sensed Mateo growing weak beside her, and she worried about his well-being.

Especially when she saw the blood streaming down the side of his face. When she saw how he grasped his bleeding shoulder.

He'd taken the brunt of that bomb—probably on purpose in order to protect her.

Emily had seen him jerk the wheel to the right. That move had ensured the explosion hit his side of the car. That she wouldn't be severely injured. Even in distress, he'd been looking out for her.

Resolve built in her.

She had to do everything in her power to ensure he would be okay.

She drew in a shallow breath as they continued to run, as they continued to try to find safety. She pulled out her phone, but there was no signal.

She'd figured as much.

How much longer until this land changed from flat into something else?

Out here, the landscape morphed so quickly.

She prayed that was the case. She needed a change right now.

They wouldn't make it if it remained flat much longer.

Mateo grunted beside her.

She glanced at him and saw his eyes press closed. His lips were pinched and his skin pale.

He was in pain.

Emily slipped his uninjured arm around her shoulder and felt his weight press into her.

"I've got you," she muttered.

But she wasn't sure how much longer she was going to make it either.

CHAPTER 38

Mateo felt himself fading.

It took every ounce of his energy to keep moving.

He knew he and Emily would be goners if they didn't.

"Look!" Emily pointed to a canyon in the distance. "Maybe we can hide there."

"Let's do that." Maybe sitting for a while would get rid of his wooziness.

Emily helped him to the gulch, and they climbed around a rock and down a small decline until they reached an old riverbed. This would offer them some shelter, some protection.

The temperatures had dropped.

Or was he cold because of his injuries?

He wasn't sure.

"We're safe . . . for now," Emily muttered as she studied his face. "But we've got to figure out a way to get you help."

"My Jeep . . . had a beacon . . . it should have alerted someone when we crashed, before it exploded."

"So, your team can trace your GPS?" Hope lifted her voice.

"In theory." He pulled his cell from his pocket and glanced at the screen. "No service out here."

He tried not to cringe. He didn't want Emily to panic.

But as she stared at him with a worried look, he knew it was too late.

She examined the wound on his shoulder and frowned. Then she pulled her flannel shirt off and pressed it into his arm. "I'm sorry. I know this hurts. But I need to stop the bleeding."

"I'm fine."

"You need help, Mateo," she murmured as she tied the shirt around him, her eyes showing a certain desperation.

"Backup will be here soon."

She touched his cheek with the back of her hand. "Your skin feels so cold."

He prayed that wasn't because he was going into shock. "I'll be okay."

She scooted to the other side of him—the uninjured side. Then she wrapped her arms around him and pulled him close.

"I promise I'm not busting a move," she murmured. "I just need to keep you warm."

"I wouldn't mind if you did, you know."

She let out a soft, almost surprised giggle. "Is that right?"

"You've surprised me, Emily Holcomb."

"You've surprised me too, Mateo Garcia."

As her body heat warmed him, Mateo leaned closer, craving the comfort.

Not just any comfort.

Emily's comfort. Her touch. Her sweet scent.

"Tell me more about you," Emily murmured.

Mateo knew what she was doing—trying to keep him lucid until help came.

It wasn't a bad idea.

Especially since his body wanted to succumb to his injuries. He wanted to close his eyes and let consciousness fade from him.

But it was better if he remained coherent.

If he wanted to keep Emily alive, he had no choice.

Emily was worried about Mateo.

Really worried. Plus . . . based on the way he was talking, he was becoming slightly delusional.

She couldn't picture him saying the things he had if he was in his right mind.

In other circumstances, it might be cute.

Right now, she was just worried.

But she had nothing to treat his injuries.

There was nothing left of the Jeep, even if they could return to it.

Plus, she feared those men might find them. Or that a wild animal might smell his blood. Or . . . Emily could go on and on about her fears, but she stopped herself.

Instead, she glanced at Mateo, hoping he'd registered her question, her request to know more about him.

"What do you want to know?" His eye lids drooped as he sagged against the rock wall.

Good. He *had* been listening.

"How did you and Rose meet?" Emily jumped right in with the question she'd been wondering about.

"She came to my family's horse ranch, and I gave her riding lessons. I was only eighteen. She was seventeen. We were inseparable after that. Got married three years later."

"Sounds like love at first sight."

"It was. Rose was a wonderful woman."

"I agree. I'm lucky to have known her. What happened to her . . . she didn't deserve it."

His muscles tightened. "No, she didn't. I failed her."

"You can't say that. It's not your fault those men did those things to her."

"I should have protected her. That was my job."

"But she wanted to fight injustice. That was in her blood, Mateo. You know that, right?" Emily turned toward him, staring at him until their gazes connected.

But he said nothing.

So she continued. "Rose was a fighter. She died fighting for what she believed in. She wouldn't change anything, Mateo. I'm sure of that."

His gaze clouded with emotion—but only for a moment—before flickering with a new thought. "You have some of that same fire in you. You know that, don't you?"

Warmth zinged through her. "If I was half the woman she was, I'd count myself fortunate."

His eyelids drooped as he reached for her cheek. "You're a good woman, Emily. A really good woman." His voice sounded raspy as he said the words.

"I try. And I'll keep trying."

A soft smile brushed his lips. "Just like Rose."

Emily stayed quiet.

Suddenly, Mateo grabbed her hand and squeezed it.

"I already lost Rose." His voice sounded hoarse as he said the words. "I don't want to lose you too, Emily."

Her heart pounded in her ears. Was this just his delirium talking?

Or did he truly mean those words?

Because Mateo was quickly gaining a place in her heart also.

After Kyle, that thought terrified her.

CHAPTER 39

 ateo wasn't sure why he was talking about Rose.

He *never* talked about her.

He preferred to keep his memories with her grounded in the happy times they'd had together. Times when they'd visited art galleries, and chased sunsets, and shared ice cream sundaes while watching their favorite TV shows.

Yet, for some reason, Mateo felt like Emily should know the truth. Should know about the events that had shaped him into the person he was today.

Rose's death had been a real turning point.

And not in a good way.

For a long time, revenge was all he could think about.

Until he realized the obsession was going to eat

him alive. Even though he'd killed Miguel Sanchez in a shootout, Mateo still found no satisfaction.

He reached into his pocket and pulled out Rose's ring. He'd kept it with him ever since it had appeared on the fence at the ranch.

He held it in his palm and opened his hand.

"What's that?" Emily asked.

"My wife's wedding ring. Someone left it at the ranch." He'd blamed himself for a long time. He'd thought he would feel better if he made the people who hurt her pay.

But he hadn't.

Vengeance didn't take away the pain, even though people thought it would. The need for more had burned inside him.

It was only when Mateo had turned back to God that he'd been able to start the healing process.

"What do you mean someone left it at the ranch?" Emily's voice sounded strained.

He rubbed his jaw. "Someone wants to taunt me."

"Oh, Mateo . . . I didn't know."

"Someone has just wanted to torment us from the start, Emily. Both of us. If they can't torment us, they want to kill us."

Emily sucked in a breath.

"Don't let them get you," he continued. He closed his hand around the ring and put it back into his pocket. "Do what you have to in order to survive."

"Don't talk like you're going to die. You're not. Do you hear me, Mateo?"

He closed his eyes again.

He wanted to succumb to his pain. To fade from reality.

But then Emily would be out here alone.

Mateo couldn't do that to her.

Instead, he pulled his gun from his holster. It wasn't a long-range rifle. But if someone came up on them, the Sig could save their lives.

He pressed it into Emily's hand. "Use this . . . if you have to."

She looked at it, her eyes widening.

"Okay?" he asked.

Finally, she nodded. "Okay."

As he heard a noise in the distance, he knew they were no longer alone.

The question reverberated: was a friend or a foe here?

Emily heard the humming noise and froze.

What was that?

Had those gunmen found them?

Would they finish her and Mateo off?

She sensed Mateo was done. That he couldn't run anymore. He didn't have the energy to do so.

But . . . that didn't sound like a vehicle. She heard no voices.

What *was* that sound?

As she looked up, a helicopter appeared on the horizon.

"Ghost . . ." Mateo muttered.

"Ghost?" Was he losing his mind? Seeing things?

"Not . . . an actual ghost . . . our pilot . . . his nickname is Ghost. He must be . . . looking for us."

Emily's breath caught. "Do you think he can see us here?"

"They're probably using a thermal imaging device. But you should . . . step out, just in case. Rocks can obscure heat signatures."

Reluctantly, Emily moved her arm from around Mateo and stood.

She stepped near the cliff and began waving her hands.

She held her breath as she waited to see what would happen next . . . as she feared the gunman might strike.

Had the pilot seen her?

She waited, praying he had.

Praying no one else had spotted them in the process.

Finally, the copter turned.

Faced them.

And headed their way.

Relief washed through her.

Help had finally arrived.

Emily only prayed Mateo would be okay.

CHAPTER 40

ateo was still sore the next morning.

Charlie had insisted he stay in the clinic area to be treated. He'd had to get several stitches, and Dr. Cossette was keeping an eye on him for a concussion.

But he knew the whole situation could have been much worse.

He was just glad that Emily hadn't been injured.

Speaking of Emily . . . she'd wanted to stay with him in the clinic, but Charlie had insisted that she get some sleep. She'd gently kissed his forehead before leaving him last night.

He could still remember the warmth from her touch. Thoughts of the kind gesture lingered with him.

But now it was a new day. Mateo had gotten some rest, despite his circumstances.

He felt a renewed sense of energy.

Mateo sat up in bed. He didn't have time just to lie around all day.

He had to find Libby.

He'd already shared with Charlie all the pertinent information about what happened, and she'd been looking into the fundraising party John had told them about.

For now, he needed to get moving.

Before he could throw his legs out of bed, someone knocked at his door.

He was pleasantly surprised when he looked up and saw Emily there.

His heart skipped a beat at the sight of her.

Skipped a beat?

That wasn't supposed to happen.

But how could it not? The woman was impressive in every way. Even though she might claim that he'd saved her life, Mateo knew if she hadn't been there to help him after the bomb went off that he wouldn't be here either.

There was something so gentle about her, something that made him want to open up. That was a feeling he hadn't experienced in a very long time.

"Hey." She offered a soft smile as she stepped inside the clinic.

"Hey to you, too." He offered a grin.

She had cleaned up since last night. Gone was the soot from her face and her tousled hair. She'd clearly showered, changed into clean clothes, and fixed her hair.

But the haunted look still remained in her gaze. "You had me worried yesterday."

"I was a little worried too. I'm thankful Ghost got there when he did."

"Me too. I'm glad you guys know what you're doing." She shifted as if there was something else on her mind. "Any updates?"

He shook his head. "I haven't heard."

Emily's gaze locked with his. "I need to find her, Mateo."

Alarm stiffened his muscles. "The best thing you can do right now is to stay here. These guys aren't playing. If they grab you again . . ."

He didn't even want to think about what they would do to her.

"I can't sit back and do nothing." Emily rubbed her neck as if her throat ached.

"You've already done a lot."

"There's nothing I wouldn't do to help someone I care about."

"That's admirable." Mateo clutched her hand, trying to get through to her. "But you're no good to Libby if you're dead."

Emily looked away as if she didn't like that statement.

Before they could talk more, Charlie stepped into the room. Based on the set of her eyes, she had an update for them.

Mateo braced himself for whatever she might have to say . . . because he had a feeling it wasn't good news.

––––––––

Emily held her breath as she waited for whatever Charlie would say.

"I'm glad to see you both are feeling better." Charlie closed the door behind her. "I know that was a rough night."

"Any updates?" Mateo got right to the point.

Charlie let out a long breath. "We're searching for the person responsible for that bomb but, of course, they covered their tracks. They were clearly watching you and knew you would be coming that way."

"And here I thought I was being careful," Mateo muttered.

"You were being careful, but these men are

desperate," Charlie said. "They wanted to send a message."

"We need to go to that party tonight," Mateo said.

Charlie shook her head, the action leaving no room for argument. "It's entirely too risky. These men have seen your face. They can identify you."

"Then who will go?" Mateo's gaze locked on hers.

She thought about it a moment before finally saying, "Hayes. He's new here so no one knows he's affiliated with us. I think he'll be our best bet."

Emily's gut tightened.

Charlie had a good point.

It wasn't as if they could just show up at the party and expect to find answers. But staying here seemed futile as well.

Maybe Hayes could discover something about Ron Howell and his wife—something that would lead them to answers about where Libby might be.

Emily prayed that would be the case.

For Libby's sake.

CHAPTER 41

After a lengthy discussion, the team finally had a plan.

Hayes would attend the fundraiser tonight. While he was there, he'd get to know Ron Howell. Ask about his house. Maybe even ask about opportunities to make some extra money in the alternative energy industry.

Mateo was certain that was a cover of some sort.

Mateo and Emily would also head in the general direction of the Las Vegas fundraiser as would others from the ranch.

Mateo preferred that Emily stay here. But she'd insisted she wouldn't.

At five p.m., they would leave.

A bad feeling brewed in Mateo's gut, but he

hoped and prayed that everything would turn out okay.

When he stepped from the bunkhouse, Emily was already waiting outside for him.

Of course.

She was anxious to leave.

She'd dressed in black jeans and a black top. Her curly hair was pulled back into a ponytail.

She looked all business.

He paused in front of her, emotions clashing inside him. He wished again that he could talk her out of this.

Despite his original intentions, he was beginning to care about her.

A memory nagged at the back of his mind.

Had he told her that when they were out there in the desert after the explosion?

He couldn't be sure.

Rose had told him once that when he didn't feel well, he tended to get chatty.

He hoped he hadn't said anything embarrassing.

He set those thoughts aside, wishing they were his biggest concern right now.

They weren't.

Mateo locked gazes with Emily, his eyes imploring hers. "Are you sure that you want to do this?"

She swallowed hard before nodding. "I've never been more certain."

That was exactly what he'd expected.

Mateo stared at her another moment before nodding. "Okay then. We better get going."

———

Emily knew the team at Vanishing Ranch didn't want her to do this. But she was determined.

It would be hard to stay in the background while Hayes searched for answers, but it seemed like a fair compromise.

Still, gut-wrenching scenarios kept racing through her mind on the drive.

What if things went south? What if Hayes got hurt? Mateo?

Or what if they were on a wild goose chase? What if they were just wasting time?

No, she couldn't think like that. She had to believe they were doing the right thing.

Mateo was fairly quiet as he sat beside her. His shoulder was bandaged. Butterfly bandages stretched across his forehead. But otherwise, he seemed no worse for the wear, despite their ordeal last night.

Occasionally, he asked a question or glanced over at her.

Emily couldn't be certain, but he almost seemed . . . apprehensive.

She had to resist the urge to squeeze his hand.

She'd known from the moment she saw Mateo the first time that he was attractive. She'd known when he rescued her that he was kind. But hearing the story about Rose brought her respect for the man to an entirely new level.

Anyone aligned with him should consider themselves lucky.

Emily didn't know what would happen once this was all over. Nor did she know what this "being over" would look like.

She hoped it would mean a happy ending for her and her sister.

Would Emily return to her old life and her position with Graves into Gardens? Would she act as if nothing had happened? That didn't even seem possible.

If this didn't finish with a happy ending . . . then Emily really had no idea what she would do.

She cleared her throat. "By the way, I researched the so-called charity this fundraiser is for."

"And?"

"It doesn't exist."

"Not surprising," he muttered.

"No, it's not. This whole event is just an opportunity for scam artists to get more money."

Several minutes of silence passed between them.

"Do you want to talk about it?" Mateo's voice pulled her from the heavy thoughts.

"I'm not sure what there is to talk about." Emily felt her nerves begin to rise. She couldn't let them get the best of her.

"Anytime you want, I'm here to listen."

She cast him a grateful smile. "I appreciate that."

His gaze lingered on her. "It's not too late to change your mind, you know."

Emily hadn't even considered doing so. "I'm definitely not changing my mind."

A frown tugged at his lips. "That's what I thought you'd say, but I had to try."

Libby's image filled her mind until a sick feeling churned inside. "I just need my sister back."

She couldn't lose two sisters. She just couldn't.

"That's what we all want. But we don't want any more casualties in the process."

She tucked her arms across her chest, trying to soothe her anxiety and keep a clear head. "I'll do whatever you ask me to. I promise."

Mateo nodded, but his jaw looked hard.

He feared the worst was going to happen, didn't he?

Seeing the apprehension on his face only reminded Emily of just how risky this whole operation was.

CHAPTER 42

Mateo drove around several minutes until he finally found a cluster of rocks to stash his car behind. The place wasn't ideal, but it should be out of the way and prevent anyone driving past from seeing them.

The rest of his team—including Jesse, Hudson, and Ainsley—had found another rocky outcropping about a half a mile from Mateo. They would be monitoring things from there.

Mateo preferred a more out-of-the-way location, but there were so few places to hide out here in the desert. He'd rather be in a more strategic position to stand guard along with his team.

But they were going to have to work with what they had.

They'd already come up with a new persona for

Hayes. He was now Hayden Black, a man who'd made his fortune in real estate back in Georgia. He wore an expensive suit, pricey cologne, and even cuff links.

Hayes had been outfitted with a hidden camera. The device was embedded on his tie clip, but the tiny lens showed them everything he was seeing. They'd seen him try it out before he left.

Emily still wasn't saying much. Instead, her eyes looked wide with a mix of anticipation and dread.

Mateo couldn't even begin to imagine what she might be going through.

He leaned back in his seat and held the iPad in his hands, watching carefully as Hayes pulled up outside a Santa Fe style mansion located on the outskirts of Las Vegas and surrounded by nothing but a fence and acres and acres of privacy. Mateo had no doubt guards were stationed around the perimeter of the property so no one uninvited could come and go.

He saw on Hayes's hidden camera that a security officer was checking IDs at the gate.

He watched, praying they didn't get derailed.

The guard nodded, handed him his ID back, and Hayes drove inside.

Mateo released his breath.

"These guys inside are cartel members, aren't they?" Emily asked.

"That's my guess. Not all of them. Some people are probably clueless."

"They say they're raising money for children, but what are they really doing?" She rubbed her arms as a tremble claimed her muscles.

"The cartel has their hands in a lot of things. Most people think it's just drugs, but they'll do whatever they can to get themselves more money and power."

"So why are they targeting us now? I hope you don't mind me saying this, but Rose has been dead for almost two years. Why go through all of this now? Is it just because I was heading to Mexico City to check on another ministry they might be involved in?"

Mateo rubbed his jaw. "My guess is that Charlie is right. Miguel's son—Diego—has taken over. He probably wants vengeance for his father's death. He blames both of us."

She rubbed her arms. "I feel like this is my fault."

He reached over and took her hand. "It's not. You can't blame yourself."

Her fingers tightened around his. "If I wasn't so stubborn—"

"If you weren't so stubborn, evil men would get

away with their selfish deeds. Never apologize for standing up for what's right."

As Mateo looked at her, all he wanted was to lean closer. To experience what her soft skin might feel like against his fingertips.

But he couldn't.

Not right now.

Instead, he cleared his throat. "Unfortunately, men like these guys think that they can get whatever they want. They feel invincible."

"I guess I should know this. In theory, I do. It's just that seeing it firsthand . . ."

"I know. It's jarring."

"And to think my sister could be there . . ." Emily absently touched the ends of her hair as she stared at the video image of the house.

"*You* could've almost been there. That's what I want to make sure never happens again." He kept his voice steady, desperate to get through to her.

Emily nodded and leaned back as if the reminder chilled her. No doubt the memories were over-whelming her.

"So now we just wait to see what happens?" She glanced at him, waiting for his response.

Mateo nodded slowly. "We wait to see if any evidence pops up. If we see your sister. Anything that tells us that we need to move in. We have no reason to believe Libby is here specifically. But hopefully Hayes can find out more information, get a better feel for these guys. I want to see their faces."

"Me too."

"And, if worse comes to worst—we're going to have to call in the FBI. I know that may not be what you want, but we don't have many options at this point."

"I understand. This is bigger than me. Bigger than Graves into Gardens."

"It is."

Emily nodded again, but her gaze showed uncertainty.

The truth was, he didn't like this any more than she did.

———

Emily kept staring at the screen, partially in awe and partially in curiosity.

She wanted to see Ron and his wife.

Wanted to know who they were up against.

Wanted to see their faces.

She needed answers, and everything seemed to be moving too slowly.

Emily continued watching the video. Watched as Hayes rubbed elbows with the wealthy in attendance. As he picked up a drink and snagged some bruschetta and some kind of shrimp tapa.

When would Hayes run into the Howells?

Ron's picture was ingrained in her mind.

Emily's best guess was that he'd married into the cartel. Maybe his wife was associated with Diego.

She wasn't sure.

As she stared at the screen, she sat up straighter.

"What is it?" Mateo asked.

She pointed. "That's him. That's Arrow."

Mateo turned up the volume as the man's face filled the screen.

"Hi there," the man said as he approached Hayes. "I'm Ron, and this is my wife, Deborah."

"What?" Mateo muttered.

"The picture Ron put online . . . it was a cover," Emily muttered. "Ron Howell is really Arrow."

"I'm running his face through the recognition system."

Mateo punched several things into his computer. A moment later, he let out a sigh.

"Here he is," he muttered. "Online, he goes by the name William Price. He clearly has multiple identities."

Mateo typed in several more things before shaking his head.

"And one more identity is Diego Sanchez. This is

our guy. Diego has been within arm's reach this whole time. He's been behind this."

"He has to be the one who has my sister."

Mateo nodded. "I agree."

"Ron Howell. William Price. Diego Sanchez. Arrow. With all those aliases what are we even supposed to call him?" Emily asked.

"Diego's his real name, so let's stick with that. Now we just have to figure out where Libby is and what this guy is up to—and I need to let the rest of my team know what's going on."

CHAPTER 43

Mateo's mind raced through what they should do next.

"Wait." Emily pointed at the screen. "It looks like they're going downstairs."

Mateo straightened. She was right.

Diego was showing Hayes around the house.

As they went down a set of narrow stairs, the screen grew darker. It became harder to see.

But maybe this was where they would discover the information they needed.

Snippets of the conversation between Hayes and Diego filled the Jeep.

"Your first time coming to one of our events?" Diego asked.

Hayes shrugged. "You could say that."

"We appreciate donations. We have prize packages we like to offer to our top donors."

Mateo's stomach churned.

"What kind of prize packages?" Hayes asked.

This was it. The moment when they'd find out the truth.

But before any of the doors in the hallway in front of them opened, four armed guards suddenly surrounded Hayes.

Mateo sucked in a breath.

These guys knew Hayes wasn't who he said he was.

His teammate was in trouble.

Serious trouble.

———

Emily's heart thudded in her chest as she watched.

No . . .

There had already been too much suffering. She prayed that these men didn't hurt Hayes as well.

Why were they even suspicious that he may not be who he claimed?

Right now, she and Mateo could only see what the camera Hayes wore showed them.

A bad feeling brewed in her gut.

"What's going on here?" Hayes glanced around as if confused.

"Who are you really?" One of the guards who'd been walking with Diego moved closer.

The voice didn't seem familiar, nor did the man's face.

"I'm a guy looking to donate to a good cause." Hayes shrugged as if it weren't a big deal. "I'm not sure what's going on here."

"We don't believe you." That same guard stepped closer, so close that all Emily could see was his black polo shirt.

Emily sensed the danger in the air.

The situation had just turned even more volatile.

"You need to start talking," the guard growled.

Hayes must have leaned forward.

Because that's when Emily saw the gun in the guard's hand.

The barrel was pointed right at Hayes's chest.

"Mateo . . ." Emily whispered.

He already had his phone out. "We're going to have to move in."

"I can—"

He turned to her, urgency in his gaze. "You have to stay here. Get down in your seat. Lock the doors. If anyone comes," he pressed something to her hands, "pull the trigger."

She stared at the weapon a moment as she tried to comprehend what was happening.

"Can you do that for me?" Mateo scooped his head lower to make eye contact.

As if she were in a daze, Emily nodded.

His voice left no room for argument.

"I'll stay here," she promised him. "You just go help Hayes."

Mateo stared at her another moment before nodding. As he slipped from the car and slammed the door, she hit the lock button.

Then she squeezed onto the floor between the dash and her seat, gripping the gun, and praying.

CHAPTER 44

Mateo grabbed his backup gun as he talked on the comm with his team.

Charlie was watching and listening to everything also, and she'd already called the feds. They were on their way.

The Vanishing Ranch team did risky things with their operations, but they couldn't lose one of their own.

Especially not in a situation like this.

He met Jesse, Ainsley, and Hudson near their vehicle.

"What do you want to do?" Mateo turned to Jesse, who was officially the leader of this operation since he had the most experience.

"We need to create a distraction so we can get

inside there and get Hayes out. But it's not going to be pretty."

"What are you suggesting?" Hudson asked.

Jesse stared at the building. "I'm thinking an explosion would work nicely. I have some stuff in my car we can use."

They headed back to his vehicle while he grabbed some supplies. Then they went to the fence and planted small bombs in four different areas.

A few moments later, they ducked behind a rock at the edge of the property.

When they were a safe distance away, Jesse detonated the explosives.

The edges of the property went up in flames.

Guards patrolling the property rushed toward the fires.

As they did, Mateo and his team scaled part of the fence that was untouched and rushed toward the house.

———

One thing people didn't often see at Vanishing Ranch was the hours everyone there put into building teamwork and training together.

Those exercises were paying off now.

As Mateo incapacitated the guard at the door, his

teammates rushed in and took down the security guards in the main house.

Women screamed. Men scrambled to leave. Everyone seemed to want to escape before the police came.

Right now, that wasn't Mateo's concern.

He watched carefully, trying to figure out the layout of the house from when he'd watched Hayes walk around.

That was how he found the door leading downstairs then rushed into the basement.

As soon as he rounded the corner, he spotted two men with Hayes.

A gun was pressed into his teammate's temple.

The look in the guard's eyes left no doubt that he would pull that trigger if provoked.

Mateo's shoulders tensed as he prepared himself to act.

He was going to have to proceed very carefully.

CHAPTER 45

Emily remained on the floor of the Jeep.

Waiting.

The seconds seemed to tick by slowly. Too slowly.

So slowly she felt as if she might lose her mind.

She kept looking at the gun she held. Imagining what it would be like to have to shoot someone. Praying it didn't come down to that.

In between those prayers, she begged God to keep Mateo safe. For her sister's protection. And for Hayes to get out of his desperate situation.

How had her life turned into such a mess? Emily usually tried to mind her own business and not make a scene over things.

But then Kyle had wandered into her life and now . . . this.

Suddenly, an explosion sounded behind her.

Light filled the sky.

Fire?

Alarm raced through her.

Was everyone okay?

She pressed down farther into the floorboard, remembering her promise to Mateo and trying to disappear in the vehicle.

With any luck, Mateo would be here soon.

That was the best-case scenario.

That's when she noticed a shadow block the full moon from the window beside her.

Someone was here.

She turned her head and looked up, fully expecting to see Mateo.

Her stomach sank when she realized it wasn't his face staring at her.

———

"You don't want to do that," Mateo said as he stared at the gun at Hayes's temple.

"You should've never come here." The gunman turned toward the other guard. "Go upstairs and check on everything. I've got things covered down here."

The other security guard hurried upstairs.

Mateo didn't recognize the man with the gun. He had no doubt this man was just a minion, working under Arrow—or Diego, as Mateo now knew him.

Speaking of Diego . . . where had he gone? He'd been down here.

Was there a secret exit that had allowed him to escape?

Most likely.

Anger burned through Mateo at the thought.

But right now, he had to focus on Hayes.

"How did you know?" Mateo asked, keeping his voice even.

They'd carefully planned Hayes's story and new persona. No one should have been able to find out.

"We have ears everywhere."

Mateo didn't know exactly what that meant. He only knew he had to keep Hayes alive. "It doesn't have to go this way."

"Why are you here?" The guard flicked his eyes toward Mateo as he pressed the gun harder into Hayes's temple.

Hayes flinched, his jaw thumping as he stood rigidly in front of the man.

Mateo had to keep this situation under control before that man pulled the trigger. "I think you know the answer to that question."

"Maybe. But I want to hear you say it."

He glanced at Hayes again. "I'll talk as soon as you let him go."

"That's not happening."

Mateo needed to get closer. From this distance, there was nothing he could do. He couldn't draw his own gun. He knew the man would reflexively shoot Hayes in response.

He only hoped his teammates would find them. But he wasn't even sure that solution would work. Down here, they'd all be cornered.

"Where is Libby?" Mateo asked.

"Who?" The man's eyes twinkled as if this were a game.

"You know exactly who I'm talking about."

"I know nothing about who you're talking about." He smirked.

"All we want is Libby, and then we'll get out of your hair," Mateo said, his hand still raised in an effort to keep everyone calm.

The man smirked again. "I'm afraid it's not going to be that easy."

CHAPTER 46

Emily raised the gun.

Mateo had told her not to hesitate before shooting.

Yet pulling the trigger didn't come instinctively to her.

That's when the man outside the car shoved someone in front of the window.

Emily gasped. "Libby . . ."

"Put the gun down or she's dead," the man growled.

Emily knew she had no choice but to do what he said.

She set the gun on the driver's seat and then raised her hands.

"Now get out," the man demanded.

Looking at the gun pointed at her sister's head,

Emily reached for the door handle and opened it. But as she started to step out, another man appeared from behind the car and grabbed her arm, knocking her off-balance. She tumbled onto the rocky dirt.

Libby gasped and tried to reach for her, but the man jerked her back.

"Stand up," the guy behind Emily demanded.

Emily rose, her gaze still on her sister. On her watery eyes. On the bruises on her arms.

"Come with me," the first man demanded. "Try anything, and you're both dead. Understand?"

She knew that this man wasn't joking.

He would kill both Emily and Libby without a second thought.

What Emily wanted to do was to hug her sister.

But she didn't dare make any moves outside what this man dictated.

She glanced around, hoping to get a glimpse of Mateo.

Was he close? Did he have any idea this was happening?

She didn't see him.

Instead, she saw cars speeding away from the estate like deer scattering at the sound of gunfire.

Maybe by the time this guy got them into the house, someone would find them.

Before that theory came to fruition, a van pulled to a stop beside them.

Libby and Emily were shoved inside.

Hoods were yanked over their heads.

Then the van pulled away so fast that Emily was thrown onto the dirty floor, her cheek smacking it so hard her entire face ached.

———

"It doesn't have to end this way," Mateo said as he stared at the gunman.

He'd been in sticky situations before when he was with the Mexican federal police. He counted himself grateful each time he made it out of a situation alive. He had gone into the job knowing full well that one day that might not be the case.

Now his job at Vanishing Ranch was no different.

But he didn't want today to be that day.

Especially since Emily was waiting for him in the car.

His only comfort was in knowing that Charlie had been informed about this.

He knew she was sending backup.

In the meantime, he prayed for his guys upstairs, that they weren't in the same situation he was.

"You shouldn't have come here," the guard growled. "We don't like strangers."

"So, you know all those people upstairs? They weren't strangers donating to your fake charity?"

The man grunted as if he didn't like his words being twisted.

A sound echoed down the steps from upstairs.

The distraction was just enough for Hayes to shove his elbow into the guard. He grabbed the man's gun with his other hand. As the two of them began to wrestle, Mateo pounced on the man's back.

His uninjured arm went around the man's throat, cutting off his air supply.

The man tried to rip Mateo's arm from around his neck. When he couldn't, he backed up and rammed Mateo into the wall behind him.

Mateo's entire body ached, but he kept pressing forward.

The man kicked, and his foot caught Hayes in the jaw.

Hayes grasped his face before righting himself again, a small growl coming from him.

Meanwhile, Mateo held tight.

How much longer was he going to have to do this until the guy passed out?

Finally, the man's body went limp.

As it did, three men fled down the stairs, guns in their hands. "FBI!"

Mateo glanced around.

Where could Diego have gone?

Had he gotten away?

He had to get back to Emily.

Now.

CHAPTER 47

"Are you okay?" Emily whispered to her sister. She'd managed to pull herself up and, despite the hood, find her sister. The two sat beside each other, shoulder to shoulder.

Libby's hand found hers, even in the darkness. "I am. But I wish they didn't have you too."

"What happened?" Emily asked. "How did they grab you?"

"There was a woman on the side of the road as I was walking home from class," she said. "I could tell something was wrong with her, so I stopped to help her. When I did, a man ran from the woods and pushed me into a car that was waiting nearby. It all happened so fast."

"Enough talking back there!" the man in the front

seat grumbled. "I don't want to hear anything for the rest of the ride."

The two of them sat on the floor of the van, still holding hands.

But neither said anything else.

Not now.

Emily had the impression one man was driving the van and another kept guard over them.

Sirens sounded in the distance.

Were the police on their way?

Emily wanted to believe the cops might track them down.

But she had a feeling these guys were smarter than that. They were probably heading in the opposite direction.

What were she and Libby going to do?

Was Mateo okay? What if these guys had done something to him also?

And how had those guys even known that she was out there in the car?

The questions swirled in her head, and despair tried to bite deep.

Right now, Emily just needed to focus on survival and keeping Libby safe.

She was going to need all her energy for that.

She would figure out the answers to those other questions later . . . she hoped.

Mateo kept his hands in the air as the FBI agent brandished his gun.

He needed to clear up his role in this—and fast.

"Hayes and I are only here to find someone," Mateo said.

"That's what they all say." The FBI agent did a half eyeroll and grabbed Mateo's arm.

Mateo's breath caught. He didn't have time for this.

"Check with Charlie Soldier," Mateo said. "She'll confirm it for you."

The agent paused and observed him. Then he glanced at the guy behind him, who nodded his approval.

Charlie carried a lot of weight. She had a lot of connections.

Mateo prayed that dropping her name would help him now.

Mateo had figured she'd been the one who'd told them what was going on, who'd sent the feds here.

The agent in front of him still didn't let him go.

So he was going to need to continue to plead his case. "Listen, I left someone out in my car, and I need to go check to make sure she's okay. I don't have time to talk this out."

The agent sighed before nodding at someone behind him. "Fine. But Agent Freeman is going with you."

At this point, Mateo didn't care who came with him. He just needed to put his eyes on Emily.

He darted up the steps and ran from the house, jogging all the way back to his car. Freeman—a middle-aged, balding man—trailed behind him.

The vehicle looked just as he left it.

But when he opened the door, the inside was empty.

Emily was gone.

His gun lay in the driver's seat.

Her cell phone on the floor.

Mateo sucked in a breath.

He glanced around outside the vehicle and spotted the tire tracks leading from the area. The ground beneath him was disturbed as if there had been a scuffle.

Somehow, these guys had grabbed Emily. Diego had been one step ahead of them and knew exactly what was going on.

How else could he explain how someone had known Emily was here?

Did they have a mole?

Mateo put the phone to his ear and let Charlie know what was happening.

He glanced at Agent Freeman. "Get in!"

They both jumped into the car and took off down the road.

He knew the chances were slim that he'd be able to track this vehicle down.

But he was going to try.

CHAPTER 48

Emily wasn't sure how long she and Libby had been riding in the van. But it felt like hours.

The road was bumpy, and she couldn't hear any noises outside, which led her to believe they were still in the desert where there were miles and miles of absolutely nothing.

They could be halfway into Mexico, for all she knew.

The thought didn't make her feel better.

As they continued traveling, Mateo filled her thoughts.

Emily wished she'd had a chance to thank him. To let him know that not only had he saved her life, but he'd helped her restore some of her faith in men.

For as long as she lived, she would never forget

him. Never forget what he'd done to help her. She only wished she'd had more time to explore whether or not their relationship could develop into something more.

She might not ever know.

"Emily?" Libby whispered beside her.

Emily leaned closer, not wanting the men in the van to hear. "Yes?"

"I'm scared." Her voice trembled.

She squeezed Libby's hand harder. "So am I."

"What are we going to do?"

"We're going to keep our heads up, and we're going to fight with everything in us to get out of this situation alive."

———

As Mateo drove, thoughts of Rose filled his mind.

Thoughts of when she'd been taken. Thoughts of the horrifying pictures he'd been sent—pictures of her suffering. Thoughts of when she'd been found— dead and in that grave.

His gut tightened.

He couldn't go through that again.

And he couldn't let Emily go through it either.

As he realized he was going nowhere, he hit the

brakes and threw his car in Park. His fist pounded the steering wheel.

The terrain had become rocky here, and the tracks eventually had led off-road. He'd tried to keep his eyes open for those tire treads. But he'd lost their trail.

That was unacceptable.

"What now?" Agent Freeman glanced at him.

"I don't know." That was the honest truth.

Why hadn't they thought to put a tracking device on Emily?

Easy—because she was never supposed to be in the middle of this.

"We can organize a party to track these guys down." Freeman held his phone, already typing something onto the screen.

Mateo appreciated the words, but he knew there was no tracking these guys down. If he didn't find them now, there was a good chance he wouldn't ever find them.

Which meant there's a good chance he might not ever see Emily again.

That thought did something strange to his heart. Not just because Emily had been a part of his assignment. But because the woman had surprised him. Had grown on him. Had made him curious and want to know more.

He hadn't really realized until this very moment just how strong his feelings for the woman were.

He'd be foolish to let her walk away without telling her how he felt.

But would he ever have that chance?

"While we wait for everyone else to help, we can backtrack and see if we can figure out where we lost the trail," Agent Freeman said. "Meanwhile, my guys have a helicopter out, and they're searching for any type of vehicle out here in the desert."

Mateo appreciated that, but he doubted it would do any good.

His muscles still tight, he put the car back into Drive and made a quick U-turn.

He would head back to check on the rest of his team. On the way, he'd look for anything suspicious that might signal where these guys had gone.

But he was nearly certain they were going to need to think of an alternate plan to find Emily.

CHAPTER 49

Mateo and his team, along with the FBI, had searched within a thirty-mile radius of the house where the gala was held, but they'd found nothing.

Several people had been arrested at the estate.

A man named Luke Maverick owned the property, but he was out of the country. According to the FBI, he seemed unaware that anything was even happening on his property. He said that the people who were there had broken in to have that party.

The FBI was looking into that explanation. But in the meantime, no one else was talking, and Diego was in the wind.

Mateo had stayed to help and add his insight, but now he and his teammates were heading back to

Vanishing Ranch. Hayes was riding with him so they could talk about the party.

Once back at the ranch, they all needed to put their heads together and see if they could figure out how to find Emily.

Before he pulled onto the road leading to the ranch, something in the distance caught his eye.

Were those lights again? Similar to the ones he'd seen before?

He called Jesse, Hayes, and Ainsley in the other vehicle and told them what was going on.

Then Mateo turned off his headlights and watched.

But the lights didn't reappear.

They had probably seen him coming and cut them.

Did they have something to do with Emily's disappearance?

He couldn't be sure.

"What are you thinking?" Hayes asked beside him.

"I'm getting a little tired of these people wandering the desert at night like they're hiding something."

"I can see that."

"I say we go find them and figure out exactly what's going on."

"I think that's a great idea."

With that statement, Mateo headed deeper into the isolated desert to see what he could find out.

———

The van pulled to a stop, and a moment later the doors opened.

Emily's heart thrummed inside her as she anticipated what might happen next.

Rough hands grabbed her and jerked her from the van. Then the hood was ripped from her face.

She looked around, expecting to be outside.

But instead, concrete walls surrounded her, walls that had been braced with huge metal beams. The whole place was cold and had a strange scent to it.

Where was she?

It looked like a large underground garage—there were no windows—with a huge steel automatic door. Two other vehicles had been parked near the entrance.

Dim lights blinked above them.

Was this part of the place she'd escaped from?

There hadn't been any lights on when she'd run.

But the scent . . . the dank, earthy aroma seemed sickeningly familiar.

Libby appeared beside her.

The guy in front of them nodded. "Follow me. Don't try anything."

Emily glanced behind her and saw a man with a large assault rifle.

She knew that trying anything would end in certain death.

She had no choice but to follow the first guy into a long tunnel. They walked until they reached another door. She and Libby clung to each other with every step.

The man at the door shoved them into a dark, cellar-like space.

At once, she realized she'd been in this space before.

It was the dungeon where she'd been kept prisoner.

The place she never wanted to see again.

"This will be your home sweet home," the man muttered. "For a little while at least."

Then the man slammed the door shut, leaving them in total darkness.

CHAPTER 50

ateo kept his headlights off as he headed in the direction of those beams he'd seen.

Driving without headlights was risky out here in the desert, but he thought he could navigate this landscape well enough.

He was about to find out.

Once he got to the base of the mountain range, he slowed.

Finally, he put on the brakes and glanced around, looking for some other sign of movement.

That's when he saw a shadowy figure dart behind a rock.

"There they are," Mateo muttered.

He and Hayes climbed from the vehicle and rushed toward the figure.

"Stop right there!" Mateo yelled.

But the man ran instead, something in his hands.

Mateo easily caught up and tackled him. The object the man was holding toppled away from them.

But when he turned the man over, he saw he was wearing a . . . lizard mask.

"You've got to be kidding me," Mateo muttered. "I don't have time for this."

He jerked the mask off the man's face, still remembering that reference that someone had made to a *Scooby-Doo* episode. It seemed to be fitting right now. If only he was in the mood to be entertained.

The man who stared back at him was the same guy Mateo had talked to at the watering hole in town —the one who'd told him about John Quito.

"You?" Mateo muttered. "What are you doing out here?"

The man raised his hands, his voice shaking. "I can explain."

"Then you need to start talking."

Hayes appeared with another man in tow, one Mateo didn't recognize.

Mateo rose and jerked the man to his feet, still holding onto his arm. He shoved him away, but drew his gun, just in case anyone tried something.

"It's not what it looks like," the watering hole man said.

"Then you need to tell me exactly what it is you're doing," Mateo growled.

"We're just looking for meteorites," he quickly insisted.

"What?"

"It's true. We just found one. It's right there." He pointed to the object he'd been holding.

Meteorites? All of this cloak-and-dagger stuff was because of some space rocks?

It didn't make any sense.

As it stood right now, Mateo didn't believe him.

There was clearly more to this story.

"You're doing what?" Charlie stared at the men wearing green cloaks and then at the lizard masks in their hands.

She'd driven out to meet them, insisting she wanted to talk to these men herself. Right now, they all stood in the desert—Charlie, Mateo, Hayes, Ainsley, and the two lizard men. Jesse had also joined them.

The headlights of Mateo's car as well as Charlie's Land Rover illuminated the area.

Mateo waited, ready to hear these men's explanation—or to tackle them if they started to run.

"I know how it sounds, but we're just looking for meteorites." Watering Hole Man—he said his name was Howey—rubbed his forehead as if suddenly anxious.

"You need to start talking." Charlie crossed her arms and gave them the stare-down.

"These meteorites that have been falling lately . . . they're special," Howey said.

"How are they special?" Charlie asked.

"Inside them, we found what's known as a hexagonal diamond."

"There are diamonds inside meteorites? I've never heard of that." Then again, Mateo wasn't an expert on falling space rocks either.

"That's right." Howey wiped his brow with his shirt sleeve. "People are paying a lot of money for them. Like *a lot* a lot. We had this meteor shower a couple weeks ago. Apparently, a lot of them fell, and we've been looking for them. There's nothing wrong with trying to make a few bucks. We're not hurting anybody."

"Then why are you coming out at night to search for them?" Mateo pressed. "That's what seems suspicious. And what's with the costumes?"

"Someone else is also hunting for these meteorites. They heard what we were doing, and we caught them following us. In fact, Walter was killed over it. It's why we had to be even more secret."

"Who's Walter?" Mateo asked.

"He was a member of our team." Howey wiped under his eyes, smearing the dirt with a mixture of sweat and tears. "We know these other guys are responsible. We just can't prove it. We told the police that also."

Walter was the man they'd found dead out in the desert, the one buried in that shallow grave, Mateo realized.

"Were you the one trying to look through the fence at the ranch?" Charlie asked.

"We thought the guys might be based out of the ranch. So we went to check it out. We never meant to scare that little girl." He shrugged. "But we had to keep wearing these masks. We were afraid if the guys saw our faces, they would come after us."

"How do you know there are more meteorites out here?" Mateo asked.

"We don't. We just want to be sure. The time and effort are worth it."

"So, you've been the ones wandering these hills for the past couple of weeks." Mateo shook his head. "Searching for meteorites."

This was a twist he hadn't seen coming.

"That's right. We've found six of them all

together. This will help pay for a place to live and for food to eat for quite a while."

"Once you find these, how do you extract the hexagon or diamond?" Charlie still appeared unconvinced.

"We have a few contacts that are into rock collecting and gem mining. They have the skills and equipment to get into the meteorites without damaging the diamonds," Howey said. "We document everything to keep it on the up and up. It's not illegal. I promise. It's innocent."

Mateo raked a hand through his hair.

This whole time, he'd thought these people might hold some answers for him.

But this had all just been a smokescreen, a distraction.

He glanced at Charlie and shrugged. "As far as I'm concerned, they're all yours."

She stared at the two men and shook her head. "They're not doing anything illegal. And you've already told the sheriff about the man who was killed, correct?"

"That's right." Howey nodded.

"Then I'd say you're in the clear." Charlie shrugged.

Mateo started to step away but then paused, realizing that maybe these guys could help. "You're out here in these hills a lot at night, right?"

Howey tensed as if he didn't like where this question was going. "That's right."

"You ever see anything suspicious?"

His eyes narrowed. "Like what?"

"Like anything going on near that gigantic home built into the mountain? The one I was asking you about when we met the first time."

He shrugged. "I don't see much going on there at the mansion. But I *have* seen some cars driving around in the hills behind it."

Mateo paused. "Is that right?"

"Yes, it's strange. One minute, I'll see them and the next they're gone. It's like they disappear into thin air."

Mateo's gaze met Charlie's.

Was this the secret entrance they'd been trying to find?

It seemed like a good chance that it was.

Mateo turned back to Howey. "Can you take us there?"

He rubbed his scraggly beard before saying, "If you promise to leave us alone after that."

Mateo extended his hand to shake on it. "It's a deal."

CHAPTER 51

Emily looked up as the door opened. She clutched Libby's arm tighter.

Diego stepped toward them. He had his stereotypical smirk on his face as he paused in front of them, appearing as if he thought himself powerful enough to control the whole world.

He clucked his tongue as if expressing comical disappointment. "All you had to do was obey."

She stared up at him, her eyes narrowed. "I won't be bullied."

He stepped closer, his fingertips brushing Libby's hair.

Emily bristled. She wanted to lunge at the man. To force his hands off her sister.

Yet she knew it would do no good. She needed to save her energy—for now.

"You won't even obey when the lives of those you love are on the line?" Diego stared at her, his finger still touching Libby's hair.

Libby's eyes widened as she waited, seeming to anticipate where he might go with this.

Seeing her sister's fear ignited something inside Emily.

"Don't touch her," Emily said through gritted teeth.

"Don't make me torture her in front of you." His grip on Libby's hair tightened, and then he jerked it until Libby let out a moan.

"Leave my sister out of this." Emily snapped. "What do you want from me?"

Diego released Libby and stepped back, appearing entirely too satisfied. "I thought you'd never ask."

He reached into his pocket and pulled his phone out. He hit a few buttons and then showed her the screen.

"All I need is for you to approve the transfer of money into my charity in Mexico," he said.

"Wait . . . that's what this is all about? I haven't approved it yet, and so now you're going to threaten my life unless I do?"

"We're waiting on more than one million dollars. That amount of money can do a lot of good."

"It can—for the people who need it. Not people who want to pocket the money for themselves." Disgust churned inside her.

"We have plans for that money. Of course, a few hundred dollars will go to the mission. We're not totally heartless."

Her hands fisted. "You're a monster."

"Maybe I am." Diego grinned before shoving the phone toward her. "So . . . what are you going to do?"

———

Mateo, Hayes, and Jesse searched near the mountain for the back entrance to the house, Howey leading the way. Howey's friend—introduced as Paul—had appeared faint, so he'd stayed with Charlie and Ainsley to drink some water until the county sheriff could come and take his official statement.

Howey remembered the approximate location of where he'd seen those vehicles coming and going. He seemed to know this area better than the average person—a fact that Mateo hoped would work to their advantage.

Wherever those tunnels were, they were well concealed. Charlie had already sent a couple of guys out here to look for them earlier in the week, and they hadn't found anything.

But if they were out here, Mateo was going to find them. Failure wasn't an option.

Jesse wandered closer to the mountains, behind one of the ridges. Their flashlights illuminated the ground as they searched for evidence—and danger.

"Hey, Mateo," Jesse called a moment later. "Come look at this."

Mateo walked toward Jesse. When he reached him, his teammate shone his flashlight on the ground and pointed at something.

Mateo sucked in a breath.

Two holes were there.

Not just holes—two graves.

Were they for Libby and Emily?

More flashbacks hit him. Flashbacks of moments Mateo would rather not remember.

Yet he couldn't forget either.

His shoulders stiffened with resolve.

He would do everything within his power to ensure these graves weren't filled with the bodies of anyone he cared about.

He waved his flashlight around the area and paused, the beam highlighting an indention in the dirt.

"Hey, guys," Mateo muttered. "I found something."

Hayes joined them. "Prints. Maybe we can follow them."

Howey paused where he was and wiped his brow again. "Listen, am I good now? I don't really want anything to do with this—I only wanted to find meteorites."

Mateo didn't see any reason to keep him. Plus, being here could put the man in danger. The last thing Mateo wanted was for an innocent man to get hurt in this process. However, Mateo did want someone to keep an eye on this man—just in case the cartel had him in their pocket.

"Hayes, can you escort him back?" Mateo gave Hayes a look, silently communicating that his team-mate should remain with the man.

"Of course." Hayes took the man's arm and led him to one of the vehicles they'd driven here.

As soon as Howey and Hayes left, Mateo and Jesse began following the prints.

The tracks weren't clearly laid out because of the rocky soil. But Mateo and Jesse still managed to follow them a hundred feet or so—all the way until they reached a small ridge.

Carefully, they climbed down and reached the desert floor.

"Where'd they go from here?" Jesse muttered as he glanced around.

That's when Mateo saw it. "Look at this."

He stepped closer to the ridge. There was an entryway big enough for a vehicle to get through. Shining his light on the ground, he saw tire tracks that led up to what appeared to be a rock wall.

But that wasn't really a rock wall.

"Are you thinking what I'm thinking?" Jesse asked.

He nodded. "There's a hidden door here somewhere—one that's been concealed with a stone facing."

He frowned.

The setup was clever. Very clever.

Unless someone knew exactly what they were looking for, this entrance would be almost impossible to see.

Now Mateo had to figure out how to get inside.

CHAPTER 52

Emily stared at the screen, knowing she had to make a decision.

She didn't want to approve these funds and then have this money go to criminals. Especially since people had sacrificed in order to make donations in hopes of helping others.

But if she sent the money now, maybe she could figure a way to get it back later. It would buy them some time. Maybe it would even save her sister's life.

Emily squeezed her eyes shut, praying she was making the right decision.

Dear Lord . . . I don't know what to do. I don't have much time to decide. If this is the wrong decision, I'm sorry.

"What's it going to be?" Diego's voice pulled her from the prayer.

With one more scowl, she jerked the phone from his hands. She punched in several things and then watched as the approval for the transfer went through.

The money was on its way to Diego's personal account.

As soon as Emily hit the Send button, failure pressed on her.

But she couldn't watch her sister suffer, not if she had a way of stopping it.

"Smart girl," Diego muttered. "Now, don't you wish you'd just done this earlier so we wouldn't have had to go through all this?"

"Now you're going to let us go?" Emily already knew the answer, but she asked anyway.

Diego let out a sardonic laugh. "Actually, I have something special prepared for you. A meal, you might wonder? Not quite. Something better."

He tapped his phone again then he showed them the screen.

Emily's eyes widened when she saw the photo of the two empty, freshly dug graves.

Libby let out a sob and buried her face on Emily's shoulder.

This was a lot for anyone to take. Emily's own mind reeled. She had no doubt Diego would follow through with his threat. Human lives were just a commodity to him.

"Well, well, well," Diego muttered as he took his phone back and hit a few more buttons. Then a satisfied smile stretched across his lips. "This just keeps getting better and better."

Emily had no idea what he was talking about, and part of her didn't want to know.

He showed her the phone again.

Security camera footage rolled across the screen.

She sucked in a breath.

Mateo.

He was standing outside in what appeared to be the desert, staring up at something.

He was here, Emily realized.

But Diego knew that too, and he wasn't going to make this easy.

Emily prayed for protection during whatever was about to happen.

———

After feeling around a few minutes, Mateo found the keypad hidden between the rocks.

"Any good guesses what the code might be?" Jesse asked.

Mateo shook his head. "Unfortunately, no."

He frowned as he tried to figure out what to do.

A sound in the distance caught his ear.

A truck.

It was coming this way.

Mateo and Jesse ducked out of sight.

They waited, watching as an SUV pulled up. A man leaned out the window and punched something in.

The door opened, and the SUV pulled inside.

Before the door closed, Mateo and Jesse ducked beneath it and slipped inside, careful to remain in the shadows. The SUV stopped and a man climbed out. He muttered something into his radio before heading to the right.

Mateo waited until the man was out of sight before turning to Jesse. "We have to split up."

They discussed their plan a few more minutes, and then Mateo texted Charlie to let her know what was going on. They were going to need backup here. But, right now, they had no time to lose.

Then they took off in opposite directions.

Just as Emily had assumed, the place was a series of dark, almost maze-like tunnels within this mountain. Some areas had dim lights that barely illuminated the space. But mostly it was dark, cold . . . and it almost felt forbidden.

Were these old mining tunnels?

Mateo wasn't sure, but it seemed like a good

possibility. He'd heard people had once mined gold in these mountains.

This was the perfect setup to smuggle things. To do things under the cover of darkness.

Mateo was sure that Diego had been doing just that ever since he'd purchased this place.

He wasn't sure which direction to head, so he went toward the house.

He was careful to remain close to the wall.

He reached the first intersection and spotted a guard standing there.

Working quickly, Mateo stepped up behind him and put the man into a chokehold.

The man struggled against him, but Mateo was patient—just like Rose had always reminded him to be.

A moment later, the man's body went limp.

Mateo released him, and he sank to the ground.

One down. How many more did he still have to go?

He remained close to the wall again as he moved deeper into the tunnel.

He heard faint voices in the distance.

He was getting closer. He was certain of that.

As he approached the next corner, a figure stepped out, blocking his way.

The man who'd been handing out flyers of Emily near that gas station.

The man's fist collided with Mateo's jaw.

The guy went in for another hit, but Mateo ducked.

As he did, someone tackled him from behind.

These guys had known he was coming.

They were ready for him. Waiting.

Mateo had known they'd have cameras set up throughout the space. But he hadn't had time to worry about that. Not when Emily and Libby were still missing.

Mateo pushed back against the second attacker and lifted his legs, jamming them into the first guy's stomach.

The man bent over, the air leaving his lungs.

Mateo was about to flip around and take on the second guy.

But before he could, something hard came down over his head, and everything spun around him.

CHAPTER 53

Emily felt her nerves thrumming with apprehension.

Was Mateo okay?

She didn't know. But she did know that Diego had a lot of his men in these tunnels. Mateo would be greatly outnumbered. Hopefully, he hadn't come alone.

The minutes seemed to tick by slowly as she waited to see what would happen.

She heard a commotion outside where she was being held. Saw Diego smiling again as if sickly satisfied.

As Libby continued to cry, Emily wrapped her sister in her arms, trying to offer comfort.

Their parents couldn't lose all three daughters.

Emily wouldn't allow that to happen to them.

She would fight with everything in her to get out of this situation.

A moment later, the door opened.

Someone pushed Mateo inside.

He stumbled before sinking to the floor beside them. Blood drizzled from his lip, and a cut stretched above his eye.

Concern pulsed through her.

"Emily . . ." he muttered.

She reached for his face and ran her fingers across it. "Oh, Mateo. Are you okay?"

"Been better."

"You didn't have to come after me." Her throat tightened with emotion.

"Yes, I did. I'll never let someone I care about suffer—not if I can stop it."

Someone I care about?

He was talking about her.

Warmth flooded her at his admission.

"Touching reunion," Diego crooned in a mocking voice. "But we don't have time for this. Sorry."

"What are you going to do with us?" Emily stared up at Diego, her gaze narrow.

"You'll see. Now the real fun begins."

———

Mateo knew that above everything else he had to protect Emily and Libby.

He was glad he'd found them. Glad to see they were okay.

But this was just the start.

He had to get them to safety somehow.

Diego crept closer, still leering down at them. "I had to make an example out of you all. My father's mantra was: we hurt those who hurt us. Besides, I can't let people think I'm weak, and that's exactly how I looked after everything that went down. *You* killed my father." He looked at Mateo then turned his pointed gaze to Emily. "And *you* brought down an arm of the cartel. I just can't let that go."

"You weren't even in charge when that happened," Emily said. "Why does it matter now?"

"I must establish my leadership. That's what my dad taught me before *he* took my dad away from me." He threw a pointed look at Mateo.

"Your father never even claimed you," Mateo said. "He didn't claim you, and no one knew you existed."

Diego's hands fisted at his sides. "It was complicated. But he did love me. I know he did."

"Why do you have my same tattoo?" Mateo asked.

"I heard about yours," Diego said. "And I wanted

something to always remember you by—especially as I plotted my vengeance. What better reminder than a matching tattoo?"

"You left that ring at the ranch, didn't you? Only it wasn't the original diamond. You planted a listening device in the ring." Mateo had figured that out when one of Diego's men had mentioned having ears everywhere.

It was the only thing that made sense.

But knowing that, he'd used it to his advantage.

He and Jesse had a key conversation before they'd come here—the perfect distraction.

Mateo was going to use the men's own weapon against them.

Diego shrugged, still looking satisfied. "I thought using the ring against you would be poetic."

"Why did you buy this house?" Mateo continued. "Why Arizona, of all places?"

"I tracked you down. Knew you were working for the ranch. As I started to poke around in this area, I discovered this house, and I knew it was perfect. Then I just had to get Emily here so I could have you both in one place."

Mateo reached for something in his boot.

They'd patted him down when they'd grabbed him. Had taken his gun.

But he expected that.

That was why he'd come prepared.

He knew there were approximately five men out in those tunnels. He'd taken down one of the men, but he could have regained consciousness again.

Then there was Diego in here with them.

Backup was on the way, but they couldn't wait that long.

He and Jesse had a plan to take them all down.

Mateo just had to make sure that nothing went wrong.

As another commotion sounded in the hallway— one that Jesse was causing, no doubt—Diego's gaze widened.

He hadn't expected another interruption.

Which was exactly what Mateo had hoped.

Just like Mateo had decided to play up the fact he'd been beaten. He wanted Diego to think that he was weak and vulnerable.

But he had other things up his sleeve.

Or in his shoe, he should say.

As soon as Diego stepped toward the door, Mateo glanced at Emily and gave her a look. She seemed to understand his silent communication of "get ready," and she straightened.

When Diego's back was turned, Mateo lunged to his feet.

He tackled Diego. As they hit the ground, Mateo's

fist collided with Diego's jaw. A few blows later, the man moaned before his eyes closed and his body went limp.

Mateo grabbed the smoke bomb from his boot. Quickly, he lit it with a lighter from his pocket and threw it into the tunnel.

Smoke filled the place, providing them a temporary screen for their escape.

Mateo turned back to Emily and Libby, knowing time was of the essence right now. "Come with me. And stay close. We need to move fast."

CHAPTER 54

ateo had planned all of that, Emily
realized.

She only felt impressed for a
moment. She didn't have time to revel in the fact.

Because this wasn't over yet.

She took Libby's hand, and they carefully scrambled over Diego's motionless body.

They ran through the smoke, keeping their mouths covered.

They'd just exited the first tunnel when someone stepped in front of them.

Someone with a gun.

Emily's eyes widened when she saw the familiar face.

Kyle.

He still looked as slick as ever with his blond hair

neatly in place, his boy-next-door face cleanly shaven, and his clothes expensive and immaculately clean—even in this tunnel.

Her stomach squeezed with nausea at the sight of the man and the memory of everything he'd done to her.

What was he doing here?

Mateo stepped in front of her and Libby.

But Emily nudged her way forward.

"You didn't think you were gonna get out of here that easily, did you?" Kyle offered a cocky grin.

Anger burned inside her as she stepped closer. "You will not keep me prisoner again. Not ever."

He glanced at her with a condescending look. Emily hadn't even recognized it for what it was until it was too late. She'd been so blind.

"I don't think you have much power here." He smirked. "Sorry."

"You need to let us go." Mateo's voice sounded at a low growl.

Commotion sounded behind them. The rest of the men were no doubt getting closer.

"I think it's honorable what a gentleman you've been to my girlfriend," Kyle continued, glancing at Mateo. "But I can take it from here."

"I'm not your girlfriend."

He smirked again. "I really did think you were

pretty great. I was sorry that what happened had to happen. But I had to prove my loyalty."

She slowly shook her head as disgust welled in her. "What are you even getting out of this?"

"I'm paid well. Very well." He shrugged as if there was nothing unusual about his choice to sell his soul for personal gain. "Now, come on. You're all coming with me."

As he took a step toward them, Mateo swung his leg.

His foot hit Kyle's gun.

The weapon fired, and the two men began to struggle against each other.

"Run!" Mateo shouted.

Emily froze.

She didn't want to leave Mateo.

But when he yelled again, she knew he wouldn't take no for an answer.

She took Libby's arm and pulled her into another tunnel. Faint lights ran along the top of this one.

When she heard a moan, she turned.

Mateo and Kyle were locked in a battle.

Kyle still had his gun and struggled to point the barrel at Mateo.

At the first chance—whenever a bullet was lined up to hit Mateo—Kyle would fire.

Emily had no doubt about that.

She glanced at the ground, looking for anything to use as a weapon. She spotted two large almost metallic-looking rocks.

One of those would work.

She picked one up.

She couldn't sit back and not do anything.

Not if she wanted to be able to live with herself.

———

Mateo saw the barrel of the gun slowly inching toward his face.

Saw Emily getting closer.

He'd told her to leave.

Why was she still here?

She raised her arms.

She held something in her hands. Something big and dark.

A meteorite, he realized.

Lifting it higher, she slammed the rock down on Kyle's head.

The man crumpled to the ground.

As he did, Mateo grabbed the gun—just in case.

Then he stepped over Kyle's body and grasped Emily's trembling arms. "Are you okay?"

"Yes." She nodded. "But we need to get out of here."

"Yes, we do."

They each grabbed one of Libby's hands and started to run.

But before they could go far, men flooded the tunnel.

"FBI! Everyone put your hands up."

Mateo and Emily froze and did as they said.

Libby simply sank to the ground.

"Diego's behind us," Mateo instructed. "He's knocked out."

As the FBI—including Freeman—rushed past them, Charlie and Jesse hurried inside.

Jesse had been setting up distractions. Had called Charlie and told her what was happening. Had let the FBI know they needed help.

Maybe this would all really be over now.

Maybe Emily and Libby would be safe, and a very dangerous man would be put behind bars and his crime ring disbanded.

As the feds took over the scene, he spotted Libby hugging Emily.

As soon as Emily stepped away and as Charlie checked Libby's injuries, Emily's gaze met Mateo's.

The two of them started toward each other and fell into each other's arms. He pressed a kiss onto the top of her head as he pulled her close.

He didn't want to let her go. And, based on the way she hugged him back, she felt the same way.

Emily hadn't ended up in that grave after all.

That was something Mateo would thank God for until the day he died.

CHAPTER 55

Emily and Libby had to stay at the site for longer than Emily wanted.

The FBI had a lot of questions.

Paramedics had checked everyone out.

Arrests had been made—Diego, Kyle, and the four other men from the tunnels.

They'd been using these tunnels to conceal their drug trade—and their plans had only been in the beginning phases. Thankfully, they'd been shut down before they could really get off the ground.

These people would do whatever it took to make themselves wealthier, and the number of businesses they had their hands in was overwhelming.

This was just the start of putting an end to their corruption, but at least it was something.

Before the paramedics had taken Kyle away, Emily had borrowed Charlie's phone.

She'd taken a picture of Kyle lying on the ground.

"What are you doing?" Mateo stepped closer and peered at the screen.

She shrugged. "Having an unflattering photo of Kyle gives me a slight amount of satisfaction. I don't plan on doing anything with it. I just want him to know how it feels. Maybe I'll send it to his cellmates in prison."

A small grin tugged at Mateo's lips. "I see."

She glanced over at Libby. Another FBI agent was talking to her now.

So she turned toward Mateo, instantly sobering as the seriousness of the situation hit her.

This place almost had been her grave.

"How did you find us?" she asked.

Mateo told her the story about the lizard man.

Emily shook her head in disbelief. "Sometimes things have a funny way of working out, don't they?"

"Yes, they do."

Their gazes caught, and she knew there was something very special between them. She thought Mateo sensed that as well.

But this wasn't the time or the place to talk about it.

They had other reasons to celebrate. But first, they had to get through this legal process.

Emily turned in time to see a vehicle pull into the tunnel. It looked FBI official.

Who was here now?

She waited with anticipation.

The doors opened and . . . her mom and dad stepped out. She'd asked Charlie to call them, to let them know Libby was okay.

Emily and Libby raced toward them and threw their arms around their parents.

Finally, they stepped back—but not far enough that their mom and dad couldn't hold onto their arms and hands. They all needed that touch, that connection, right now.

Dad's gaze locked with Emily's. "You said you'd find Libby, and you did. But I was afraid we were going to lose both of you."

"I knew you were praying for us through it all," she said, her voice cracking.

They hugged again. Then her dad looked over her shoulder and paused.

He stepped toward Mateo and extended his hand. "You are a man of your word. I don't know how I could possibly ever thank you for that."

Mateo shook his hand. "There's no need to do that. I'm only glad everyone is okay."

Dad put his arm around both of his girls. "And so are we. You have no idea."

EPILOGUE

s the doorbell rang, Emily took off her apron and quickly pushed a few stray hairs out of her eyes.

Flutters filled her stomach as she walked to the front door.

As soon as she pulled the door open, a huge smile lit her face.

Mateo stood there wearing jeans and a white T-shirt, a bouquet of cheerful peonies in his hands.

His smile matched hers. "Good evening, *mi cariña.*"

"Good evening."

He handed her the flowers. "These are for you."

"They're beautiful. Thank you." She took them and breathed in their aroma a brief second before extending an arm behind her. "Come in."

He stepped inside, and Emily closed the door behind him.

As soon as she set her flowers on the table beside her, Mateo stepped closer. His eyes were warm and proudly displayed his affection.

His arms circled her waist as he pulled her close.

Emily's pulse raced—just as it did every time they embraced.

She rose on her tiptoes, and their lips met.

They'd been dating for the last four weeks—ever since Diego had been arrested.

And these past four weeks had been the most wonderful of her life.

Mateo was real. Imperfect.

And everything she wanted.

"I've missed you," he murmured when they stepped apart.

She rested her hands on his chest. "I've missed you too. But I did make some dinner for us—my famous lemon chicken piccata."

"It smells wonderful."

"I was hoping you'd like it."

"I'm sure I will. Next time, I'll make you some of my family's pozole."

"Pozole?" The dish sounded familiar, but Emily had never had it before.

"It's a soup. I like to serve it with sliced radish on top. I think you'll like it."

She grinned. "I can't wait to try it."

The two of them had been splitting their time together. Emily visited him one week, and Mateo visited her the next. So far, the arrangement had worked out well.

Emily grabbed his hand and led him into the kitchen.

They paused near the island, and Mateo turned toward her. "How's your family?"

"Libby is doing really well. She's back in school and going to counseling, just to be on the safe side." Emily was also getting counseling, working through everything that had happened. "My parents are busy keeping an eye on us a little more than necessary. But that's to be expected. They told me to tell you hello."

"Tell them hello also. I look forward to seeing them at Thanksgiving next week."

"They're looking forward to seeing you too. And . . . I have more good news."

"What's that?" Mateo tilted his head as he waited for her response.

"Graves into Gardens was able to get all the money back—the money that was transferred into Diego's account during my duress. Those funds will go toward people who actually need it now."

"That's fantastic!"

"I think so too. That, coupled with the fact that Tucker was arrested in Mexico and will be locked up for a while, is a nice conclusion to this mess." She paused and crossed her arms. "But there *is* one thing that's been bothering me."

"What's that?"

"Who was that man who set me free?"

Mateo twisted his head. "That's a good question. We don't know. You said you didn't recognize this guy's voice during the FBI raid, right? You don't think he was in the bunker when you were there the second time."

"That's right."

"There's a whole network of the cartel still out there. I suppose he could be in the wind."

She pressed her lips together. "Maybe."

But she had a feeling there was more to this guy's story. She might not ever know what it was. But she was thankful for his courage when he'd let her go.

"What about that mock town that was set up in the basement of that house?" she continued. "Did you ever hear anything about it?"

"Only that the man who built the house was a prepper. He was preparing for doomsday, and he wanted to set it up so that, in the event of an apocalypse—or anything remotely resembling that—his family could try to maintain a semi-normal life."

"The things we do for the people we love, right?"

"We do everything we can to protect them, that's for sure." Mateo peered over her shoulder at the food simmering on the stove. "That looks tasty."

Instead of responding, Emily nestled closer to him as he leaned against the counter. He tucked his arms around her waist again as they peered at each other.

What they had between them felt so natural.

She was thankful God had brought Mateo into her life—although the circumstances to get them to this place had been less than favorable, to say the least.

She and Mateo now had an agreement. Whenever she had to travel out of the country, he would be her new bodyguard. She liked that idea. She *really* liked that idea.

Whenever Mateo was with her, she felt safe, as if he was a shield that surrounded her.

It was a feeling she treasured, especially after the ordeal she'd been through.

He pushed a curl from her face as he peered down at her. "You're beautiful inside and out. Have I told you that before?"

She lifted a shoulder as she felt warmth flush through her. "Maybe a couple of times."

"It's true."

She reached up and brushed her fingers against his jaw.

Without saying anything else, she planted another kiss on his lips.

A soft kiss that turned into more.

God had turned the worst part of her life into something beautiful. He'd turned betrayal into loyalty. Grief into hope. Despair into celebration.

He had a way of doing that.

And Emily couldn't wait to see what else the future held . . . what others had intended as graves had become the foundation for beautiful things instead.

~~~

Thank you for reading *Lethal Betrayal*. If you enjoyed this book, please consider leaving a review.

Keep reading for a preview of *High Stakes Deception*!
~~~

CHRISTY BARRITT

High Stakes
DECEPTION

VANISHING RANCH **VR** THE SERIES – BOOK SIX

HIGH STAKES DECEPTION: CHAPTER ONE

As Ainsley Tatum sat in her car staring across the street at Carter Winslow's stately brick home, she considered backing out of this assignment. Leaving. Pleading conflict of interest.

But if she'd been able to bring down cartel members when she was a Texas Ranger, then she was certainly capable of facing the man who had broken her heart all those years ago.

She glanced up and down the sunbathed Denver, Colorado, street as the stakes of this assignment slammed into the forefront of her mind.

Carter's father, Doyle, had been killed in a suspicious car accident almost a year ago. Ainsley didn't believe it was an accident.

In fact, she and her team at Vanishing Ranch had

been investigating a terrorist bombing in Florida from fifteen years ago—a bombing that had killed her brother, Jason, who'd been interning for a US senator at the time.

They'd found a trail of US citizens connected with the event. Their evidence indicated that someone powerful—or a group of powerful people—had planned the event and framed international terrorists in order to cover their tracks.

Their working theory was that Doyle had discovered the involvement of several people he'd done business with. When these men learned Doyle knew too much, he'd been permanently silenced.

Ainsley and Carter needed to uncover the truth without raising suspicions. They would pose as newlyweds in order to meet with one of those men under the guise of exploring a business proposition.

Ainsley's nerves thrummed inside her at the thought.

So much was on the line right now—and she wasn't even talking about her heart.

However, she had to get moving. Jack Earl, her number one suspect, was expecting Carter this evening. She didn't want to be late and miss any opportunities.

As she reached for the handle of her SUV, Carter's front door opened.

She paused and watched as a beautiful woman stepped onto his porch.

Ainsley's gaze darkened.

Of *course.*

Even though she and Carter were supposed to be newlyweds, he'd still found time to entertain another woman—and possibly blow their cover in the process. What if Jack had men watching them? Didn't Carter know they needed to be careful?

The woman with him now looked like just his type. Tall and slender with dark hair, refined features, and an impeccable taste in clothing.

So maybe Ainsley wasn't *totally* over what happened between them.

But that was silly. She was a grown woman. She should be able to put the past behind her.

Carter certainly had.

With that sobering thought, Ainsley kept watching.

Carter stepped outside behind the woman. Handsome, handsome Carter with his tousled blond hair, striking blue eyes, and broad shoulders. The man was both handsome and brilliant. He'd developed software that cut back online identity theft by fifty percent.

Two years ago, he'd sold his company, and Ainsley's understanding was that he no longer had to work. Yet he was still involved in the tech field, using his intelligence as a private contractor on whatever projects he chose.

Ainsley watched as Carter and the woman laughed together. Then he leaned toward her, kissed her cheek, and the woman turned to leave. Her high heels clicked on the immaculate shrub-lined sidewalk as she made her way to a BMW parked in the driveway.

Ainsley released a long, pent-up breath.

She should just call her boss, Charlie Soldier. Tell her that she needed to find someone else for this assignment.

In fact, that's what Ainsley would do. She didn't have to put herself through this emotional turmoil. She didn't have anything to prove.

She grabbed her phone from her purse, ready to make the call.

Before she dialed any numbers, she looked up once more and watched as the woman opened her car door and climbed inside.

As Ainsley's fingers hovered over Charlie's number, an explosion filled the air.

———

Carter heard the blast. Saw the flames. Felt the heat gust across his face.

He watched in horror as fire consumed Maureen's car.

No . . .

"Maureen!"

She'd just climbed inside. Maybe it wasn't too late to get her out.

He prayed that was the case.

Shielding his face with his arm, Carter darted toward her vehicle.

Reaching it, he tried to grab the handle.

The heat was nearly unbearable.

As the flames seemed to shrink for a moment, he saw his opportunity.

He grabbed the handle in one last attempt to save her.

Heat blistered his skin, and he jerked his hand back.

The flames were too high, too intense. The fire engulfed the entire vehicle.

He couldn't even see Maureen through the flames.

But he couldn't just stand there!

He started to reach for the door again when someone jerked him back.

"You can't save her!" a high-pitched voice shouted. "It's too late."

As the horror of what was happening washed over him again, he couldn't tear his gaze away from the car. He had to do something!

He started to reach for the door again.

Before he touched it, the person beside him rammed her shoulder against his abdomen.

Tackled him to the ground.

As his body collided with his grassy lawn, another explosion ripped through the air.

The gas tank, he realized. The flames had reached the gas tank, causing another blast.

Carter sat up and ran a hand over his face, hardly able to comprehend what had just happened.

"Maureen . . ." he muttered.

This couldn't be possible.

The heat from the blaze scorched his skin as sirens sounded in the distance.

His gaze remained on the burning car as the truth settled into his chest.

Maureen couldn't have possibly survived that.

"Carter . . . I'm sorry," a soft voice said.

A voice that sounded familiar.

A voice that instantly swept him back to the past.

He glanced beside him, and the air left his lungs when he saw the figure staring at him.

"Ainsley?" He choked out the word.

He hadn't seen her in years. *Years.*

But he'd thought about her often.

Too often.

If possible, Ainsley Tatum looked better today than she had sixteen years ago. She'd always been tall and thin, but now curves graced her body in all the right areas. Her straight, honey-blonde hair and smattering of freckles gave her a wholesome girl-next-door look.

But her eyes weren't nearly as innocent as they'd once been.

No, they were filled with experience. Grief. Maybe even pain and regret.

Ainsley stood, wiped the grass from her jeans, and then she helped him to his feet. "The police are on their way. We don't have much time."

He stared at Maureen's car again as the fire continued to burn.

An ache panged in his chest.

"I'm sorry about your loss," Ainsley continued. "But it's too late to rescue her. Your friend is gone. The blast killed her immediately."

Carter knew that. But he didn't want to accept it as the truth.

He rubbed the skin between his eyes, hardly able to process the scene before him. He'd just been chatting with Maureen. Telling her about how he truly believed there was a time for everything and a season for every activity.

He hadn't expected to be confronted with her death so quickly after the proclamation.

Ainsley grabbed Carter's arm and shifted him until he faced her. Then she locked her gaze with his, clearly trying to drive home a point.

"Listen, Carter," she started. "If we're going to sell our story, we need to start pretending. Now. As far as anyone is concerned, you and I just got married."

His mind blanked as he tried to comprehend what she was saying. "What?"

"Come on . . ." She tilted her head. "Charlie went over all this with you."

He squinted, still in a state of shock. "Charlie? Charlie Soldier?"

Ainsley stared at him another moment as if he'd lost his mind. "Yes. Of course, I'm talking about *that* Charlie."

He raked a hand through his hair, not caring if he left it standing on end. He needed to shake off his shock and try to focus.

Was that even possible?

He pressed his eyes closed as he thought through

the situation. "Wait . . . *you're* the one Charlie sent from Vanishing Ranch? You and I are supposed to pretend to be married?"

What kind of joke was this? Everything about it was a terrible idea. *Terrible.*

Confusion raced through Ainsley's gaze. "I thought Charlie told you."

"Charlie only told me she was sending one of her operatives. She didn't give me a name. Doesn't she know that you and I," Carter wagged his finger back and forth between them, struggling to find the right words, before he finally finished with, "have a past?"

Ainsley planted her hands on her hips as she stared up at him. "I told her. But she insisted on sending me. She said we're both professionals. When the police get here, we're going to tell them we just got back from a month-long trip to Mexico where we met each other and spontaneously eloped. Got it?"

Carter's eyes widened, but he nodded.

That would be a little easier considering the fact he truly had just gotten back from Mexico. No doubt, Ainsley knew that.

Having Ainsley help him find the truth threw a whole different spin on the situation.

They were supposed to act like newlyweds.

Him. Ainsley.

What were the odds?

He eyed her again, thankful for the distraction from the burning car. Maybe.

But there was still a lot he didn't understand.

"I thought you were a Texas Ranger," he finally said.

"I was. I'm not anymore."

Carter wasn't sure what to think of this.

Things hadn't ended well between them. Ainsley had refused to listen when Carter tried to explain his side of the story. It probably wouldn't have mattered what he told her—she wouldn't have believed him. She'd been too angry.

Maybe he deserved that. The situation had been complicated, to say the least.

As two cop cars squealed onto the scene, Ainsley thrust something into his hand. "Wear this."

His breath caught when he looked down and saw a wedding ring.

Quickly, he slipped it on. Glancing at Ainsley's hand, he saw she already wore one.

Their charade was now official.

Carter glanced back at Maureen's car one more time.

His heart thudded with grief as he tried to process this loss.

Was Maureen's death somehow connected with his father's death? With Jack Earl?

Determination hardened inside him.

Carter would figure it out if it was the last thing he did.

Click Here to Keep Reading

COMPLETE BOOK LIST

Squeaky Clean Mysteries:

   #1 Hazardous Duty

   #2 Suspicious Minds

   #2.5 It Came Upon a Midnight Crime (novella)

   #3 Organized Grime

   #4 Dirty Deeds

   #5 The Scum of All Fears

   #6 To Love, Honor and Perish

   #7 Mucky Streak

   #8 Foul Play

   #9 Broom & Gloom

   #10 Dust and Obey

   #11 Thrill Squeaker

   #11.5 Swept Away (novella)

   #12 Cunning Attractions

   #13 Cold Case: Clean Getaway

#14 Cold Case: Clean Sweep

#15 Cold Case: Clean Break

#16 Cleans to an End

While You Were Sweeping, A Riley Thomas Spinoff

The Sierra Files:

#1 Pounced

#2 Hunted

#3 Pranced

#4 Rattled

The Gabby St. Claire Diaries (a Tween Mystery series):

The Curtain Call Caper

The Disappearing Dog Dilemma

The Bungled Bike Burglaries

The Worst Detective Ever

#1 Ready to Fumble

#2 Reign of Error

#3 Safety in Blunders

#4 Join the Flub

#5 Blooper Freak

#6 Flaw Abiding Citizen

#7 Gaffe Out Loud

#8 Joke and Dagger

#9 Wreck the Halls

#10 Glitch and Famous

Raven Remington

Relentless

Holly Anna Paladin Mysteries:

#1 Random Acts of Murder

#2 Random Acts of Deceit

#2.5 Random Acts of Scrooge

#3 Random Acts of Malice

#4 Random Acts of Greed

#5 Random Acts of Fraud

#6 Random Acts of Outrage

#7 Random Acts of Iniquity

Lantern Beach Mysteries

#1 Hidden Currents

#2 Flood Watch

#3 Storm Surge

#4 Dangerous Waters

#5 Perilous Riptide

#6 Deadly Undertow

Lantern Beach Romantic Suspense

Tides of Deception

Shadow of Intrigue

Rocco

Axel

Beckett

Gabe

Lantern Beach Mayday

Run Aground

Dead Reckoning

Tipping Point

Lantern Beach Blackout: Danger Rising

Brandon

Dylan

Maddox

Titus

Lantern Beach Christmas

Silent Night

Crime á la Mode

Dead Man's Float

Milkshake Up

Bomb Pop Threat

Banana Split Personalities

Beach Bound Books and Beans Mysteries

Bound by Murder

Bound by Disaster

Bound by Mystery

Bound by Trouble (coming soon)

Vanishing Ranch

Forgotten Secrets

Necessary Risk

Risky Ambition

Deadly Intent

Lethal Betrayal

High Stakes Deception (coming soon)

The Sidekick's Survival Guide

The Art of Eavesdropping

The Perks of Meddling

The Exercise of Interfering

The Practice of Prying

The Skill of Snooping

The Craft of Being Covert

Saltwater Cowboys

Saltwater Cowboy

Breakwater Protector

Cape Corral Keeper

Seagrass Secrets

Driftwood Danger

Unwavering Security

Beach House Mysteries
The Cottage on Ghost Lane
The Inn on Hanging Hill
The House on Dagger Point

School of Hard Rocks Mysteries
The Treble with Murder
Crime Strikes a Chord
Tone Death

Carolina Moon Series
Home Before Dark
Gone By Dark
Wait Until Dark
Light the Dark
Taken By Dark

Suburban Sleuth Mysteries:
Death of the Couch Potato's Wife

Fog Lake Suspense:
Edge of Peril
Margin of Error
Brink of Danger
Line of Duty
Legacy of Lies
Secrets of Shame

Refuge of Redemption

Cape Thomas Series:
Dubiosity
Disillusioned
Distorted

Standalone Romantic Mystery:
The Good Girl

Suspense:
Imperfect
The Wrecking

Sweet Christmas Novella:
Home to Chestnut Grove

Standalone Romantic-Suspense:
Keeping Guard
The Last Target
Race Against Time
Ricochet
Key Witness
Lifeline
High-Stakes Holiday Reunion
Desperate Measures
Hidden Agenda

Mountain Hideaway

Dark Harbor

Shadow of Suspicion

The Baby Assignment

The Cradle Conspiracy

Trained to Defend

Mountain Survival

Dangerous Mountain Rescue

Nonfiction:

Characters in the Kitchen

Changed: True Stories of Finding God through Christian Music (out of print)

The Novel in Me: The Beginner's Guide to Writing and Publishing a Novel (out of print)

ABOUT THE AUTHOR

USA Today has called Christy Barritt's books "scary, funny, passionate, and quirky."

Christy writes both mystery and romantic suspense novels that are clean with underlying messages of faith. Her books have sold almost four million copies and have won the Daphne du Maurier Award for Excellence in Suspense and Mystery, have been twice nominated for the Romantic Times Reviewers' Choice Award, and have finaled for both a Carol Award and Foreword Magazine's Book of the Year.

She is married to her Prince Charming, a man who thinks she's hilarious—but only when she's not trying to be. Christy is a self-proclaimed klutz, an avid music lover who's known for spontaneously bursting into song, and a road trip aficionado.

When she's not working or spending time with her family, she enjoys singing, playing the guitar, and exploring small, unsuspecting towns where people have no idea how accident-prone she is.

Find Christy online at:
www.christybarritt.com
www.facebook.com/christybarritt
www.twitter.com/cbarritt

Sign up for Christy's newsletter to get information on all of her latest releases here: **www.christybarritt. com/newsletter-sign-up/**